Wild Ride
The Wild Brothers
Book 2

Tory Baker

Copyright © 2024 by Tory Baker

All rights reserved. No part of this book may be reproduced in any form or by any electronic or mechanical means, including information storage and retrieval systems, without written permission from the author, except for the use of brief quotations in a book review. No part of this book may be used to create, feed, or refine artificial intelligence models, for any purpose, without written permission from the author.

Please respect the author and do not participate in or encourage piracy of copyrighted materials that would violate the author's rights.

This is a work of fiction. Names, characters, businesses, places, events, locales, and incidents are either the products of the author's imagination or used in a fictitious manner. Any resemblance to actual persons, living or dead, or actual events is purely coincidental.

Cover Design by LJ with Mayhem Cover Creations

Editor Julia Goda with Diamond in the Rough Editing

Photographer by Katie with Cadwallader Photography

Models

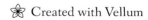 Created with Vellum

The strength of a woman is not measured by the impact that all her hardships in life have had on her; but the strength of a woman is measured by the extent of her refusal to allow those hardships to dictate her and who she becomes.
-C. JoyBell C.

Blurb

Fletcher Wild wants the one woman he shouldn't go after.

She's my boss's daughter.
She's off-limits.
She's going to be mine.

I wasn't prepared for Delilah Taylor. Settling down was never on my radar. Almost getting caught with my mouth and hands on her body were definitely not in my plans. Now that I've had a taste of her, I'm rethinking every single f*cking thing.

Tory is bringing you Fletch's story. You saw him help his friends in the Wild Johnson Brothers. Now, it's Fletcher's turn to fall fast and hard! This man in uniform isn't afraid to use his handcuffs when it comes to making Delilah his.

Prologue
Fletch

Three Days Earlier

Delilah Taylor is a temptation a man like me doesn't want or need. I'm not the settling-down type, or I wasn't. I've left that to a few of my brothers. I'd much rather stay single and continue going after the next thrill. Whether it be in the form of working undercover, bungee jumping off a bridge, sky diving—and I've done it enough not to need a tandem partner—or swimming with sharks. Still, the light-blonde-haired beauty with blue eyes, lush lips, and a smattering of freckles along her nose and cheeks is hard to deny.

I had one taste of her lips, felt her body pressed against mine as her soft pomegranate fragrance permeated the small area surrounding us. Fuck, I can still remember her scent days later. Delilah went to my head faster than my next adrenaline rush; never mind the preferred liquor I like to drink. Only the noises of the police station put a stop to our time together. My hands were fisted in her hair, she had her legs wrapped around my waist, and my cock was rock fucking hard pressed up against her center.

Delilah Taylor is meant for fantasies, *my* fantasies. I'm talking in the shower with my hand wrapped around my length or in my bed when no one is around, and I can remember exactly how she feels. The woman who has my guts wrapped in knots is off fucking limits in the worst way possible. She's my boss' daughter. A boss who just so happens to be the police chief. I knew he had a daughter. Fuck, the whole town did. She's younger, wasn't on my radar until he updated the picture he has on full display on his desk. Still, she hadn't come to the station since she left for college, and I wasn't prepared for the up close and personal welcome I received. Our heated moment was interrupted by Delilah's dad calling her name and mentioning to the other police officers he wanted to introduce her to the newer deputies.

The small *oops* that escaped her mouth made my dick instantly deflate. We'd barely exchanged glances before I was going after her. Never in my life did I act like a dog in heat with so much as a look and a lingering touch. I also didn't think I'd be helping the damsel in distress when Delilah was attempting to open the supply closet. The attraction hit me like a ton of fucking bricks; it also had me shaking my head in disbelief. She scurried around me, acting like she wasn't rubbing herself along my body only moments ago. She was so close to coming, another minute or so and I'd have had another memory to jack my cock to.

I did what any smart man would do: I kept my hands to myself and got out of town the very next day. *I fucking ran.* Luckily for me, I had a lot of hours banked over the course of the year. The chief of police's daughter—only I would have that kind of luck in our too small town of Peach Springs, Georgia. There isn't another police station within a decent amount of time from our family homestead, let alone my own house.

Now that I've been gone a few days, maybe coming home won't be so bad. And yeah, I ran away like a fucking coward with his tail tucked between his legs. I couldn't trust myself to be around Delilah. The attraction is too fucking strong, and wanting to keep my job is too fucking valuable. I hopped on a plane and flew to Wyoming, where my buddy Lawson Johnson and his family live. A perfect opportunity for clearing my head, to help them out with an issue his younger brother had with a rogue fucking veterinarian. It's always something with that clan. Hell, the same could be said for my own brothers. Luckily, none of them have come calling asking to get out of a speeding ticket or anything else lately.

What I wasn't prepared for was stepping off the plane in our small rural airport and my phone ringing the minute I turn the thing back on. I look down at the screen and see it's my boss.

"Hello, Chief," I answer, holding my breath.

"Hey, Wild, are you back in town?" he asks, cutting to the chase. Chief Taylor calls all his deputies by our last name. What I'm wondering is why he's calling to ask me if I'm here.

"Just got off the plane. Everything okay at the station?" I figure it's work even though I'm not on the clock until tomorrow.

"Yeah. Delilah is stuck on the side of the road with a flat tire. I'm two hours away, and she can't get the damn lug nuts loose." Fuck me, fuck this, fuck everything.

"Send me her number and where she's broken down. I'm walking toward my truck now." I can't necessarily say no. Even if Taylor weren't my boss, I'd never leave a woman stranded on the side of the road, especially with the sun setting over the horizon.

"Thanks, I appreciate it. I'd ask one of the others, but I'll be damned if I trust them." Yeah, that doesn't make me feel any better because clearly I can't be trusted where Delilah Taylor is concerned either.

"No problem. I'll have her call you when she's up

and running." We get off the phone rather quickly, and the time away I've had to get my head on straight was all for nothing. I know myself better than anyone—a few minutes in Delilah's presence, and I'm going to be doing a whole lot more than changing her tire. I'm fucked, well and truly. At least I'll die with the taste of Delilah on my tongue. The minute Chief Taylor gets wind of one of his employees fooling around with his one and only daughter, shit is going to hit the fan, and I'll be lucky to come out alive.

Chapter 1
Delilah

Present Day

"Ugh." The last person I should be thinking about is Fletcher Wild. So what if his touch is permanently seared to my memory? Not to mention his scent. I swear the slightest combination of lemon, cedarwood, and mint, well, my knees are trembling as I'm tossed back into a memory I've been trying to avoid.

Maybe if I bury my head in the sand, it'll keep my mind off the man who pretty much wined, dined, and sixty-nined me on the side of the road after saving me from my flat tire. Fletch did me a solid. He helped me out when no one was around, coming to my rescue like the poor damsel in distress from a princess movie. Only his parting gift was an orgasm of all orgasms. He literally ruined me for every other person, including myself. Yep, even my own fingers and toys are no longer doing the trick. I am absolutely one hundred percent pitiful.

"What did your car ever do to you, sweet pea?" I've only just slammed my door shut, looking down at the tire. The tire that got me into all this trouble in the first place. It's the fault of a massive piece of metal I happened to run over. As much as I tried to avoid the culprit, it was impossible. Oncoming traffic on one side and a ditch on the other meant there was no other choice. Thankfully, there was an intersection coming up once the *thump, thump, thump* of my tire had me slowing down and driving as carefully as possible.

"It's more like what it didn't do to me," I respond, looking up at my dad. He's in his standard uniform shirt, badge around his neck, hat on his head, gun at his waist, black denim jeans, boots that have seen better days, and his hands on his hips. The dad pose of all poses. He hasn't changed much over the years. Dad is a creature of habit and despises all things change. Mom and I make fun of him every chance we get, a man of routine through and through. Even now he's standing the exact same way as all those funny video clips talking about their dads, only he has a bit of his police chief title thrown into the mix.

"Yeah, your mother mentioned you were stuck having to buy two new tires. How much that set you back?" I grumble. I really don't want to hear what he has to say, even if he's right. This is dad's same old song and dance. *'You should have bought this car instead of what you're tooling around in.'* Well, I wanted to be impractical. There was no need for a big, massive, armored vehicle that Dad would prefer his only daughter drive. My two-door Lexus RC 300 about gave Dad a heart attack when I pulled up in the driveway after I finagled one hell of a deal.

"I don't want to talk about it." This is the first time in a year I question myself about my fire-engine red car. Tires, oil changes, and routine maintenance on vehicles are absurd, no matter what the make and model of your car is. The up sale they tried to pull on me was of little to no use. I can change my own air filter, windshield wipers, and even put air in my tires. Needless to say, I replaced two tires because of the wear pattern, paid a mint, and saw myself out of the dealership the second I could.

Dad lets out a whistle. "Should have stuck with something easier to maintain, Delilah."

"How long have you been holding that in?" I'm really not aggravated at the cost of my car. I work hard to afford what I want in life, even if it does set me back more than I'd care to admit at times.

"Quite a damn while." I'm sure the reason for his salt and pepper hair turning grayer by the day has a lot to do with the two females in his life. Mom and I are a force to be reckoned with. We look alike, we talk alike, and we act a lot alike, too. We also march to the beat of our own drum. You can't tell us what we're doing is wrong even if it's true. What can I say, we're the type of people who have to learn from our mistakes, much to his chagrin.

"I figured. Hey, Dad, I have a question for you." I'm probably showing my hand when I shouldn't, but it's been a few days. A few days that I've driven by the station on my way to run an errand, going a bit out of my way to look for his truck like a freaking stalker. I'm not this person, not usually, but when I tell you his dick has me hooked, I am hooked. Fletcher Wild also has a personality women dream of, dark brown hair mixed with shots of blond from the sun, warm green eyes that can change in intensity depending on what is going on around him, taut muscles, and the man has no problem holding you after knocking your socks off.

"Yeah?" He brings me into his side with his arm wrapping around my shoulder.

"Fletch, is he around? I'd like to thank him for helping me out of the jam I was in earlier this week." Not a complete and total lie, maybe pushing the truth a bit. Luckily, I know how to keep my body language loosey goosey, or Dad would see right through me.

"He's out for the week. The town is putting together a memorial for his parents, and he asked for some time off." Well, damn. Now I feel worse. Here I am, thinking with my vagina, when everyone knows the Wild's parents were taken tragically by a car accident. It was all too soon, and they were way too young to lose family like they did.

"Ah, well, I'll have to figure something out to thank him," I suggest, poking the bear into giving me some useful information.

"Hmm, not sure what he'd like. Your mom might. She brings all kinds of stuff to the station."

"Thanks, Dad, I'll ask her and go from there." I give him a sideways hug and start to open my door when he steps in front of me.

"Anytime. Don't be a stranger at the dinner table this weekend, okay?"

"I'll be there." I had to work one weekend, and he's yet to let me live it down. I'm a freelance accountant. Numbers are my thing, plus I like to work for myself, which means sometimes your hours are when you make them.

"I've heard that before." He holds the door open until I slide into the seat.

"Once, I've missed a dinner, and you're going to hold it over my head. Wasn't it you last time who missed it?" I joke with him.

"You got me there, sweet pea. Drive safe, and I'll see you soon." My finger hits the push start button on the ignition, we finish our goodbyes, and I've got a game plan set in motion.

Chapter 2
Fletch

Damn, I was hoping this year would be the year I wouldn't drink myself into a fucking stupor. Since the day I turned eighteen, you could find me taking the day off, sitting on my back porch overlooking the trees with a bottle of whiskey in my hand, taking long and deep pulls until it was empty. When I wasn't home, I'd continue my journey into self-destruction wherever my feet landed. It didn't matter the location as long as I had solitude. I allowed myself one day a year to mourn the loss of our parents. Six boys left behind when they were too damn young and taken away from us too fucking soon.

Asher and Beau asking me to meet them at the bar with the news of our parents having a monument of sorts donated in their name twenty years later, and grief still has the power to allow the darkness to creep inside. We had a few drinks. I had more than my brothers, and I damn sure didn't drive. I sent a text to the Chief the next morning to let him know it would be another few days until I'd be back at the station. I'm fortunate in the sense of the word that I've yet to take a long period of time off except a day or two here and there, or I'm sure he'd have told me to get my ass to work. Now I'm hanging at home until I feel like I'd be worth enough to actually work. They brought me back home the other night, where I continued drinking. It was my own fault to be suffering the consequences of my own actions. I'm old enough to know better but still too young to care.

I'm giving myself one more day before I'm going back to work. Something has to give to keep my mind off the shit swirling in my head. I damn sure can't keep my thoughts away from what it means to be front and center of the memorial being honored in our parents' name. I get it's a good deed—they did a lot for the community—but having to be around more than my fair share of people, rehashing all of the good memories and remembering how we lost it all? No fucking thanks. Then there's Delilah, her taste, her touch, her soft moans against my ear, and I'm instantly ready to say *fuck it* and damn the consequences, but there are two things holding me back: her father, my boss, and the fact she's made for settling down.

"Christ," I mutter under my breath. Her name

alone has my dick lengthening inside my sweats. Maybe today would be a good day to get out of the house, except I'd probably run into the one person I'm trying to run away from. It looks like it's going to be another cold shower, except I know nothing will help. I'll end up with my hand wrapped around my cock while replaying taking Delilah on the side of the road. Luckily, where she pulled over was in a deserted area, nothing but trees for miles on end. And with it going from dusk to full-on darkness, it meant we were secluded. Delilah's hands were on the hood of her car, bent over at the waist, and I was fucking her with my fingers, hard and fast. She liked the way I whispered into her ear exactly what I was going to do to her, making her come on my fingers, waiting until she could no longer hold herself up, and was then draped across the warm metal. The only way my cock was going inside of her was with her looking at me, watching the entire time as I fed her my cock inside her tight pussy.

A knock on the door has me biting back a curse, probably a good thing, but tell that to my dick, who misses Delilah as much as I do. I stand up from my place at the bar, head throbbing as much as my cock. I'm barely on my feet when the knocking stops and then starts up again.

"Fuck, someone better be bleeding out. I'm coming." That's the problem. I'm not. I have a headache, my dick is hard, and I'm a miserable human being at this moment.

"Okay." I hear a voice that isn't Beau's or Asher's. Nope, it's a voice that haunts me. Light and rich while being warm and bright depending on the moment. Truth be told, I like when she's moaning my name while her center clenches down on my length the best. I'm at the door faster than I planned, not understanding exactly why Delilah is here in the first place.

I open the door, unprepared for my eyes to land on the beauty before me, and any chance of my cock settling down is long gone. Delilah is holding up a platter of sorts, her arms pushing up her tits, and damn if I'm not pissed my mouth and eyes weren't on those the last time we were together. Her blue eyes change from light to a velvet color when she sees what I'm wearing. My cock flexes beneath my sweats, and her gaze zeros in on it.

"Delilah, what are you doing here?" I take in her long blonde hair hanging in loose waves and the slight tinge of color on her cheeks that travels the length of her neck toward her chest. She licks her lips, her tongue remaining out for a moment more than normal, and it's got me fantasizing of all the ways I want to see exactly how she'd use it on my cock. The way this woman makes me feel, you'd think I'm addicted to her and sex.

"Well, um... I wouldn't be here, except you haven't

been at the station and, uh, I brought you cookies to say thank you for the other night." She's in another one of those floral sundresses she's worn the last two times and now a third. The thin straps on each shoulder are tied in a bow, and the fabric is form-fitting around her tits and waist before flaring out around her hips and thighs.

"Chocolate chip?" I question. My mouth is salivating for a fuck ton more than the plate of cookies she's offering.

"Of course, I hear that's your favorite." My manners have been thrown out the window. I've yet to invite her in, and there's a reason for that. The minute she crosses over the threshold, my mouth will be on hers, I'll be ripping up the flimsy excuse of a dress she's wearing and pushing my sweats down until my cock is free. There wouldn't be a need to see if she is as wet for me as I think she is. The past two encounters we've had together have proven she's more than ready for me. Then I'd slam inside of her wet depths, fuck the condom, fuck the repercussions we'll surely face.

"Not sure those are my favorite anymore." Delilah is picking up what I'm putting down, going so far as to take another step closer to the doorway. "Woman, you come inside, you won't be leavin' until you're too damn sore to move, let alone walk," I warn her off. The way I'm feeling, the way she's looking, there's no way I'll be able to keep my hands or dick to myself. Delilah isn't heeding my warning. Nope, it seems like she's after the same exact thing I am. I watch as she moves the plate to one hand. Her other goes to my chest, but she doesn't keep it there. This fucking temptress slowly drags the palm of her hand lower and lower.

"Is that a promise?"

"It's a guaran-fucking-tee." My hand slides around her waist, and I pull her inside. Delilah Taylor may be my demise and salvation all wrapped in one delicious package.

Chapter 3
Delilah

"Shit." I'm barely through the door when the platter of cookies is starting to slip. Fletch's quick thinking has him grabbing it from me. How he's managing to do multiple things at once, I'll never understand, not while his mouth is attached to mine. The moment the plate is taken away, I'm all over him. My hand continues its path, slowly sliding down his thick muscular stomach, feeling each peak and valley of his abs. Fletch's lips on mine, his tongue licking my lower lip, the soft mewl leaving me makes him nip at it with his teeth. The tips of my fingers meet the waistband of his sweats, and every meme or video you've heard about a man wearing gray sweatpants is true, at least for Fletcher Wild. The outline of his thick and heavy cock had me some type of way. I was ready to throw caution to the wind and quite literally climb him like a pole. He's a shower while also being a grower. Some men could never be as lucky as Fletch or, well, me. I'm the only one reaping the rewards.

"Oh my god," I breathe between each word when my hand wraps around his length. I'm ashamed to say that I've seen his cock, felt him inside of me, but have yet to touch his dick. A complete and utter travesty I will never let happen again.

"Christ, Delilah," he groans, his mouth leaving mine and moving to my neck, where he nips at me once again. It's plain as day he likes to bite, and what it does to me is out-of-this-world amazing. I slowly start to work my hand up and down, twisting my wrist as I go. "Tighter," he all but demands. His hand slides beneath my dress, grabbing a handful of my ass as he walks us backwards. The door is now shut, and my back meets the cool wood. It does nothing to calm down the desire building up inside of me. I do as he says, holding him with a firmness I'd have thought it would hurt, but apparently, that's not the case for Fletch.

"Fletcher." It looks like we're not ever going to make it to a flat surface, you know, like a bed. Walls, the side of the road with me holding on to my car for dear life, and now my back is pressed against the wall. "Please, more," I beg, feeling his fingers move closer to my center from behind. My body trembles with need. Why is it always like this when we're near one another? The all-consuming need to be naked and have him pushing his cock inside me, it's the only thing I can think about.

"You gonna make me come, Delilah?" Two fingers drive inside me, causing my head to tip back, giving Fletch more room to nip, suck, and lick at the column of my throat. "Woman, you get me off with your hands, I won't be coming inside you." His words only spur me on while I continue working his shaft. Our breaths become even more heated when I sweep my thumb over the head of his cock, gathering his precum to use in order to keep up my pace. Fletch antes up the stakes, as if we're playing a game of Texas Hold 'em, trying to beat who can make the other come first. We both already know who's going to win.

He will. Always.

"Fuck, yeah, want your cunt wrapped around my cock, feel this wetness without anything between us." His admission sends a shockwave to my core.

"I'm not on birth control." God, how I wish I were right about now, but being celibate meant not bothering. I knew my cycle like clockwork. I've yet to miss a period and can tell you the day when it'll start.

"Fuck." The four-letter word is my sentiment exactly.

"You can pull out," I offer as I lose his fingers. I'm ready to kick and scream, except Fletch wraps his hands around mine and rubs the blunt tip of his cock along the lace of my thong.

"Woman." It's a gamble, one I'm willing to take.

"I've never, you know." A look like I've never seen before crosses his face.

"Never gone bareback, Delilah." My thong is ripped off my body. Now there's nothing between us. "Be sure. I'm not going to be able to stop once I feel your tight-as-fuck cunt tightening around my cock."

"I'm positive. Fuck me, Fletcher, take me. I trust you." My hand leaves his length, as does his.

"Watch. Look at us." It's a command, and I obey him without thinking anything of it.

"Fletch." My pussy stretches around his thick length. Seeing my wetness coat him has me ready to close my eyes, and I almost lose sight of us, but I've come to know Fletcher Wild. He'll pull out of me, make me wait until my eyes are back where he wants them, and only then will he give me what we both need.

"The next time I take you like this, it'll be in front of a mirror. It's too fucking hot to miss a moment." He bottoms out inside of me, hitting a spot, that spot, one that feels almost painful yet doesn't. I take a deep breath, and he must feel the exact same thing because his body locks up. "Fuck, woman, you're killing me. So tight, so hot, so fucking wet."

"Move, please. I need more." I'm desperate, no longer able to keep any pretense of watching as he manages to work my body up by staying so still. My head tips back as I swallow and grind my hips downward to spur him into action.

"Goddamn it, Delilah. Off." I'm not sure what he's asking for until he's pushing up my dress, and all I can do is lift my arms, then Fletch takes care of the rest. The minute I'm completely naked, his head bends downward as his fingers entwine with mine, holding them at either side of my head, and he's pulling a nipple into his mouth. It's an onslaught of sensations, overwhelmed with how he is able to maintain his composure as he strokes in and out of me. On every upward thrust he swivels his hips, and his pelvis hits my clit in the most delicious way imaginable.

"I'm close." I'm unsure of how he's going to be able to pull out with the way my pussy is clamping down, my orgasm hitting me faster than it did on the side of the road. A feat I never thought would be possible. Anyone could have seen us. The thrill of getting caught hit me fast, but that was nothing compared to this moment. His hard velvet shaft without a barrier feels indescribable.

"Fuck, yeah, get there, Delilah. I'll pull out and

paint all this beautiful fucking skin with my cum." He pulls away from my nipple before moving to the other, this time nipping it with his teeth. That's all it takes, and I'm soaring. Eyes closed, my hand ripping away from his to dig into in his dirty blond hair, holding him to my breast while my legs are locked around his waist.

"Fletcher." His name tumbles from my lips on a gasp. He doesn't stop. He keeps fucking me through my orgasm and yet somehow manages to hold himself back.

"Damn it, I'm not ready to leave your tight cunt," he croons into my ear. It sucks that I've lost his mouth on my nipple, but having him talk me through my orgasm is so much better.

"I don't want you to leave. I want to feel you, Fletch. All of you." I'm an idiot for suggesting he come inside me. Pregnancy is a lifetime commitment.

"Woman." He sucks on the skin beneath the shell of my ear.

"The timing isn't right." I've already calculated the days in my head while trying to coax him to let go.

"When was your period?" He plants himself inside me in one hard thrust.

"A week ago." Fletch moves harder, faster, and somehow deeper. We maintain eye contact this time. My body starts to free-fall again. Only this time, I'm pulling Fletcher right along with me. Never in my life have I been able to come twice, back to fucking back.

"Damn, Delilah," he grunts on an exhale as I feel him come inside me, and I'll never want to have Fletch any other way. Which is going to be hard during certain parts of the month, so either we go back to condoms, or I get on birth control, as soon as possible.

"Yeah." I'm speechless. The only thing I can manage to do right now is feel.

"Christ, that's sexy as fuck," Fletch says, then he pulls out, dropping to his knees, and I feel our combined cum leak out of me, painting my thighs. What I don't expect is for him to drag his fingers through the wetness and push us back inside me. "Never gonna want you any other way. Though maybe next time, we'll make it to a bed." My fingers linger in his hair, combing through the mussed tendrils, and I let out a small laugh.

"That'll be a first."

"Fuck, yeah, it will be." He stands, pulls his sweats back up, and lifts me in his arms. "Right now." It's then I feel his cock.

"Already?"

"Took you hard, Delilah. You too sore to go again?" He ignores his dick.

"Nope, not at all, but this time, I want to use my mouth," I whisper into his ear. He walks us to what I'm sure is his bedroom, and I feel him the entire way. I think it's safe to assume he likes the idea of me sucking him off.

"Turnabout is fair play. While you swallow me, I'm going to eat your pretty pussy." I know Fletcher is going to make good on his promise, and I'm going to enjoy every moment I have with him.

Chapter 4
Fletch

Delilah is draped across my chest, completely wrung dry. I'd have thought she was asleep if it weren't for her moving every once in a while. Her legs are tangled with mine, we're skin on skin, and I'm finding I love having her soft pomegranate scent wrapped around me. I'd take her again if my cock weren't fucking limp for the first time since I've been around Delilah and she weren't sore. After I ate her pussy and she sucked my dick dry, swallowing my cum like she promised, we took a brief intermission for food: sandwiches, chips, and her chocolate chip cookies were as good as it was gonna get in the way of dinner. She didn't seem to mind, both of us ravenous from missing lunch.

I swear coming inside this woman, she'll be the only woman who gets that from me. Never in my life did I think I'd take a woman without a condom. Delilah Taylor has me questioning my theory on the no-strings-attached sermon I've been preaching. Call it trauma from losing our parents at a young fucking age, but I never wanted to do something similar had I settled down. Now here I am, wrapped around a blonde-haired temptation. One who could have me losing everything I've ever worked for—my job, my purpose, and my name.

"Fletch?" Delilah lifts her head from her place on my chest.

"Hmm," I respond, pulling her closer to me. Her wet cunt on the outside of my thigh has my cock ready to perk up. Too bad I'm too damn tired. He'll have to wait until we've taken a nap.

"Shhh, I can hear you thinking." She moves her fingers from my chest, where she was drawing patterns, to my lips, holding her pointer finger in place to keep me from talking. "Don't ruin my post-orgasmic haze by talking about reality. Let me have this for a bit longer."

"Message received, loud and clear." My hand grips her fingers, and I place a kiss on them, watching as she nods then settles down on my chest again.

"Good, there's a lot to unpack. It can wait. We have plenty of time."

"Not sure that's the case. Someone told you my favorite cookies; I'd be willing to bet it was your mom.

Which means she's not an idiot and knows you came over here."

"Fine, we'll do this now." She sits up, causing the sheet to drop to her waist, and my hand reaches out to palm a tit, thumb rasping over her cherry-tipped nipple. Technically, if I keep my hands on her, I'm not ruining our day. Hell, I'd much rather have this conversation with her riding my cock. I don't think that will happen today, though, not with how she winced when I pulled out earlier. "I'm well aware my father is your boss. I'm also twenty-eight years old, I have my own place, I pay my own bills, and who I have sex with shouldn't be anyone's business. Least of all my parents'. That being said, we live in a small town." She takes a breath. I do an ab curl to sit up and watch the desire blossom in her eyes.

"Legs." I tell her, my hands wrapping around her shapely hips. Christ, there I goes giving us a chance to take a breather. I know the minute her pussy is near my cock, I'll be lifting her up until I'm notched inside her wet depths.

"This won't be difficult or anything." Instead of plunging inside her, my thick cock lies along her slit. Should we need to break things up from the heaviness of this conversation, I've got not one single problem with fucking her.

"Try." My head dips into the crook of her shoulder

and neck, where I breathe in her scent of me, sex, and pomegranate. She smells like mine.

"Fine, as I was saying, small town. My dad is the chief, yada yada. We'll play this out in whatever way you would like. I understand you have more to lose than I do. This is your career, and as much as I love my father, I'm not exactly sure how he would take us seeing one another."

"There is that. I'm leaving this up to you, Delilah. I can't necessarily take you bareback and ask you to keep us hidden. Then again, there could be the chance he fires me, and I'll have to find a new job somewhere else. Either way, we'll make it work, yeah?" It's hitting her pretty clearly what could potentially happen. This thing between us is new, the sex is off the fucking charts, and the rest we'll work on. Relationships take work. I saw it firsthand—slow dances in the kitchen, making dinner when time allowed it, Mom and Dad working hand in hand together in every way imaginable. Sure, they had their fair share of fights. They also made up and showed us brothers how it's done. My own fears are leaving my wife and kids too fucking early, especially since I'm a cop.

"Okay, fine. For starters, since you were bareback inside me, this is exclusive." I arch an eyebrow at her, letting her know that's a fucking given, but just in case, I'm telling her, too.

"Woman, since the moment you marched your

sexy ass into the station, all I saw was you, no one else. Not before, not during, and definitely not in the future."

"Good. I'm going to get on birth control." For some reason, I don't like the idea of that. A vision of her pregnant with my child, a slight bump to her belly while she's sitting like this has my dick throbbing with the need to fuck my kid into her before she goes to the doctor. Except I'm not that much of a dick where I'd take the choice away from her.

"Fine with me." I somehow manage to keep my tone cool as a cucumber when my gut is churning in the opposite way.

"Alright." Even Delilah's voice sounds like she's questioning her statement.

"What else?" My hands are firm on each of her hips, my lips moving along the underside of her jaw, ready to take her and fuck the rest of our worries away.

"I'm leaving that up to you, Fletch. This is your life, too, not just mine." Christ, she undoes me. Delilah should be thinking about herself more than me. I can handle whatever is thrown my way. She, on the other hand, the last thing I want is her dad to be pissed at me and take it out on her. Though, I doubt that would be the case. It's one of those catch-22 deals. You never know what someone is capable of.

"How about this? For now, we keep this between the two of us. You come over here whenever. I'll keep my hands to myself whenever you're at the station. I can't guarantee it in public, though. My woman likes the thrill of getting caught, and I aim to please. That being said, this goes the way I think it will, you won't need birth control, your father won't need a reason to shoot me, and you'll be right where you belong." I lift her up and slam her down on my length. She shudders for a moment but then adjusts.

"God, yes. Right where I belong." My mouth attaches to hers. Delilah slides up and then down, setting the tempo on how this goes. And I can tell she needs this nice and slow.

"Fuck, yeah, I'm gonna come inside you again, Delilah, then we're going to take a nap, and I'll wake you up with my head buried between these sweet-as-hell thighs," I promise her, knowing I'll make damn good on it, too. Tomorrow, I'm going back to work, which means I won't have her here at my place like I do right now. The next time will be when I'm off work, and with me taking an extended absence, who knows how long that'll be.

"Fletch." The way she says my name so sweetly, it's going to take everything I have to take her nice and slow. Yet I know I'll do it for *her*.

Chapter 5
Delilah

The blaring of an alarm jostles me from my sleep. The heavy arm wrapped around my body tightens its hold a second after the noise is silenced. I keep my eyes closed, not ready to face the day ahead of us. There wasn't a whole lot of convincing needed in order for me to crawl into bed and sleep the night away. I was tired, sore, and happy even if we're keeping this to ourselves until we're on solid ground. That was the compromise at least. I mean, there's something to be said about feeling so in tune with a person. Never have I felt the connection with a man that I feel with Fletch.

"A man could get used to this." His husky voice skates across my neck, his lips rasping my skin. The hair from his beard does even more delicious things to my body, including causing my thighs to clench together.

"So could a woman." I roll over to face him. I'm sure I've got bedhead, morning breath, and wrinkles on my face from sleep, but I don't care. I want to see what he looks like first thing in the morning.

"We'll make it happen as often as possible." My nose slides along his, and his lips land on mine. Our kiss is soft, sweet, and over before it gets hot. Probably due to the fact his alarm is going off again.

"You're one of those, aren't you?" I pull back, teasing him for the alarm.

"Yep, not one to wake up unless there are at least three timers set, and that doesn't include the snooze button." My face must give me away, because Fletch lets out a throaty laugh, and it has me doing the same.

"What time do you have to be at work?" I ask. Being a freelance accountant means I can start and end my day when I want. It also gives me room to be a bit too relaxed if I'm not careful. I've done that twice since I've been home and had to pull all-nighters in order to play catch-up.

"In an hour." I lift my head off the pillow, looking at the old-school style clock, one reminiscent to what my parents have in their room—brown, rectangle, with bright red numbers and what I'm sure is a massive snooze button on top that's easy to hit. I calculate the time it'll take him to get to the station. There's no time for anything besides him getting ready. Damn that kind of sucks.

"You better get moving. I'll make coffee and find some breakfast," I offer, hoping I'm not messing up his morning routine.

"I'd appreciate that, though I'd prefer you in the shower with me," he grumbles as if he's put out by the thought.

"Rain check?" Fletch's lips brush against mine one last time before he's up and out of bed, unperturbed by his state of nakedness first thing in the morning. The man has absolutely nothing to be bothered about. He's sex on a stick, has the swagger to go with it, and, well, if I were a man and had what he has between his legs, I would walk around naked, too. I'd probably also swivel my hips and see exactly how much fun a man has to work with.

"Absolutely," Fletcher says, looking over one of his broad shoulders. Add his thick arms, a waist that is muscular but not overly so, an ass that begs you to pinch, and thick thighs, and yep, now I'm going to need a shower of a different kind, a cold plunge to put my overactive hormones to rest.

I scramble off the bed, pulling the sheet with me while I hunt for the discarded shirt Fletcher gave me last night to put on while we wait.

"Found it," I mutter under my breath, shaking it out before pulling it on. My clothes are still in a pile by the front door. Neither of us bothered cleaning up after ourselves, not clothes and definitely not the food. Which means I'm going to have to work fast, a hard task when it comes to leaving Fletch's bed. It's like a cloud hugging you in sheer comfort. Then there's the scent of him surrounding me as well what was his body. I uncross my legs, place my feet on the rich hardwood floors, and scamper out to the kitchen. Socks probably would have been a smart move, or a pair of slippers to combat the chill in the morning. Fletcher's house really is beautiful. The color of the floors and walls, the textures from the couch and rugs, the way the early morning sun shines through the windows. It may be a little sparse in the way of furniture and personal belongings, but it's cozy feeling. Fletch would probably be mortified to walk into my apartment. I'm pretty sure I have every shade of pink you can imagine in some way, shape, or form. I may have what most would consider a boring job; that doesn't mean I don't have a spice for life.

The short hallway opens up to the living room and kitchen. I veer to the left. The coffee pot will take the longest whether it's to heat up for a single coffee pod style or to brew a full pot. Truth be told, I much prefer the old-fashioned style, the stronger the better, and no matter what I do on one of those single style machines, it doesn't cut it.

"Jackpot. I don't know why I thought any differently." I get to work, taking the carafe to the sink, filling it up with water, and surveying what Fletch has in the fridge and pantry. My eyes flit to the clock on the stove. Time is limited, so making a big breakfast is out the window today. Maybe next time I can make him a bagel, egg, and cheese sandwich. Today, it'll have to be my special concoction of a lightly toasted bagel, a light layer of butter, topped with a good smear of cream cheese with a cup of coffee. I get lost in working my way around in his kitchen. Realizing I'm going to be drinking my coffee black makes me want to cry. I'm a cream-no-sugar kind of girl, and having to do the opposite does not make me happy. I doctor everything up when I realize I have no idea how Fletcher takes his coffee, so I keep the sugar out of the equation but put a healthy amount in mine. Then I finish the bagels, putting them on one plate and using my other hand to hold two piping-hot cups of coffee by their handles.

"Don't spill, don't spill, please don't spill," I say a little mantra as I head back toward Fletcher's bedroom. I'm shuffling my feet instead of taking full steps, worrying the coffee will slosh over the side of the mugs and burn my hands. Luckily for me and Fletch, he doesn't have a massive house. I'd probably be up shit's creek without a paddle. Especially if he had a two-story house with a master on the top floor. Me and stairs are not friends. I learned that lesson when I was a teenager at my grandparents' house. A broken arm and badly bruised tailbone from running up and down the stairs with my cousins taught me a valuable lesson. Sadly, it's one that has stuck with me, and till this day, I will be overly cautious when at the rare occurrence I have to use them.

I enter the bedroom and stop abruptly in my tracks. Fletcher is standing in the doorway of the bathroom, hands up and resting on the frame, wearing nothing but a towel, and I nearly swallow my tongue. A tremble works its way up my body. The mugs clinking together spurs Fletch into action.

"Woman." He pulls his bottom lip into his mouth with his teeth. My eyes eat him up with every move he makes toward me. I have no idea where to keep my gaze. He pulls me in without so much as a whisper of a touch. "You're going to burn yourself. Don't do something like that again, especially when I can easily help." My hands are divested of the cups of coffee, and Fletcher puts them on the dresser, uncaring that the heat could ruin the wood, before he repeats the process with the plate.

"I had it." Probably not the best response, but you look at a man like the one before me and try to formulate a full sentence.

"Yeah, you do have it, Delilah." We're not talking about what I was carrying. "I take your mouth right now, I'll be late for work, and after taking time off, the last thing I can be is late." I glance at his alarm, noticing that time is dwindling down, and move to sit on the dresser in preparation of watching Fletcher's every move.

"Alright." His hands go to my hips, helping lift me up on the dresser, then he proceeds to give me the show I've been waiting for. My hand reaches for my mug of coffee, and I take a sip while I watch every step of Fletch getting ready for work. He drops his towel, not in the least bit abashed by his state of undress, and it's clear as day I'm not the only one feeling the need to feel him between my legs again. What I don't expect is to enjoy the show of Fletcher Wild getting dressing in his uniform. As a little girl, when I watched my father do similar, it was with hero worship and stars in my eyes. As I got older and noticed the dark circles beneath Mom's eyes, I knew the reasoning. We all did. He'd kiss us both goodbye, and maybe he'd come home after his shift, maybe he wouldn't. There was always a piece of me that said I'd never put myself in the same boat as my mom. Except I'm watching Fletch step into a pair of denim jeans, then grab his uniform shirt, all crisp lines and with his name attached to it. The shirt does not wear him; he wears the shirt. And now I know without uncertainty that there's no denying it'll be me up pacing the floors late at night when I'm waiting on Fletcher to come home. My thumb goes to my mouth, and I nibble on my nail, nerves starting to take over.

We haven't even said *I love you* to one another, yet I can already feel them ready to slip off my tongue.

"You good, Delilah?" He takes me off guard after he buttoned up his shirt.

"Me? Yeah. Actually, I probably should be getting ready, too." I move to hop off the dresser, my stomach in knots, but he blocks my path. Thinking about loving and losing someone in the same breath isn't for the faint of heart.

"Stay as long as you want. I'll leave you a set of keys. You can come and go as you please."

"Are you sure about that?" I ask.

"Yep." He's direct and succinct in his statement.

"I'll make you a key for my place, too." Fletch tilts his head to the side. He's about to say no, so I do what I always do when it comes to getting the last word in. I place my finger on his lips and say, "I know things will be tricky right now, but one day, you'll be able to use it, too." His hand finds my wrist, pulling my finger from his lips, and he nips at the tip. He doesn't respond with words. Instead, he steps closer, kissing me into silence and telling me in a different way he likes my idea.

Chapter 6
Fletch

I was late for work. Not that we have a set time to be in the office. Once my ass hits the seat in my police-issued SUV and I turn the ignition, I'm on the clock. Still, it would have been nice not to be the last deputy to walk into the building on a random weekday.

"Hey, Wild, good to see you back," the receptionist greets me as I walk through the glass doors. I've got a to-go cup of coffee in one hand courtesy of the blonde bombshell who had me re-thinking coming back to work. The heavy make-out session did nothing to calm down the semi I was sporting all morning, and the only reason I pulled away from Delilah was because the woman was trying to climb me like a tree. Any other given time, I'd have said *fuck it* and bore the consequences, except I heard the small hiss of pain coming from her. My male ego was ready to thump my chest with fucking pride. I did that, wore her out so she's feeling me hours later. The other was pissed because she was in pain, and that also meant I'd either have to take it easy with her, or her pussy would be off limits. Fuck, that is the last thing I want. I've become intoxicated and addicted to her in every single way.

"Hey, Susan." I wave at her with my unoccupied hand. "Did I miss anything?"

"Nope, it's been a pretty quiet week. You know what that means." Her lips tip up in a smile, but her facial expression tells another story.

"This weekend is going to be hell on earth," I finish for her.

"You've got that right. Glad to see you're back all the same." No one would come out and say anything, yet when one guy is out, it makes the schedule a bit tighter around the station. We all work more hours than scheduled. Shit happens. We've all had to pull a double, holidays are just another day, and the only way most survive is through overtime. Especially the guys who have families. The pay is shit for what we do. We do our job because we love it, plain and simple. For whatever reason, each of us is pulled in this direction for a cause of our own, whether it be a family generational thing, wanting to help due to a traumatic event, or any other given reason. I'd wanted to be a cop when I was a youngster. I'd play with my brothers, making them be the robbers so I could arrest them. It only made me want to become a cop that much more when the news was delivered about how our parents died. On the cusp of teenage hood, a shit ton of hormones and rage running through my blood had me veering off the right path. I wasn't into anything illegal, but I was all about partying and not settling down. Hell, even the thoughts of ever finding my forever woman weren't on my radar. The past week has me changing my ways, and it's all due to Delilah.

I got the smallest taste of her and started to rethink my ways. My parents loved each other so much that if one of them survived, it would have slowly killed the other, and we'd have witnessed them die slowly. Back then, none of us were thinking about anything but our grief. Almost twenty years later, I understand that while losing them fucking sucked, both of them going together was ultimately better, even if that's a hard pill to swallow.

"Thanks. Hopefully, I won't take any more time off for a while." I keep to myself on those dark days, and no one is the wiser, minus my brothers on the rare occasion when I need a ride.

"We all deserve to have days off, Fletcher. You shouldn't have to work yourself to the bone to live." Susan is a wise one. She's also around the age my mother would have been.

"Then shouldn't you be practicin' what you

preach?" I lift an eyebrow in question. She huffs out a puff of air and rolls her eyes.

"Honey, a few more years, and I'll be walking around in shorts and sandals. Retirement is going to look good for this old lady." She takes a sip of her coffee, then the phone rings, and Susan enters work mode. The same damn thing I should be doing. My head is everywhere except in the game. I'm going to have to screw it on straight and stop fucking around, or I'm going to find out.

I continue my walk toward my desk. With Peach Springs being a small town, there are only a few of us on duty at the same time. The station is pretty quiet. Wyatt, one of the other deputies, is on the phone, saving me from having another conversation and giving me time to settle in. George, must be out on patrol, probably a good thing since my place is going to be at my desk for the foreseeable future in order to get caught up. Joseph, Michael, and Dom are here during the night shift for the next few months, then we'll rotate. That's the shit part of the job. It's not the paperwork that's a pain in the ass. It's getting into a new routine, finally settling in and then switching up again.

"Jesus." I pull my chair out as I look down at the mounds of files on my desk. It's going to be one of those days. My coffee is nearly finished, and sadly, the sludge in the breakroom is too damn nasty to drink. There's strong coffee, and then there's coffee that puts hair on your chest. Indigestion is not an additive I'm ready to throw into the work week. I take a seat in my chair, power on my computer, and start sifting through what's on my desk. It's not like me to leave my work unattended, but seeing as how I met up with my brothers after work, figuring I'd be at the station the next day, I didn't bother taking any files home. Now, I'm going to be glued to this fucking place for however long it takes, stuck with shitty-ass coffee.

"Wild," Chief Taylor says my name just as I'm about to start working through the mountain of a mess on my desk.

"Chief Taylor." We might have all come to know each other through the years, but one thing you don't fuck around with is addressing him correctly or messing with his daughter. Since I can smell Delilah lingering on my clothes, I'd say I'm well and truly fucked if he moves any closer or asks me to come to his office.

"Someone's getting canned," Wyatt jokes like he's got room to talk.

"The only person who's going to get canned is you, Brewer." Taylor makes his way toward our desk.

"And with that, I'm outta here." He stands up like the flames of hell are licking at his heels. Wyatt has had a few fender benders since he's taken the job here. Nothing major, and none were his fault, but that doesn't mean he doesn't take a beating for it either.

"Later," I say. Taylor nods and walks closer to my desk.

I figure it's do or die, so to speak. Chief Taylor, much like the rest of us, can sniff a liar out a mile away. The mannerisms in which people portray themselves, the lack of eye contact, crossing your arms over your chest, fidgeting, and a slew of other tells give us a clear indicator. Which is why I've got to be on my A-game. There's no way I'm ready for the confrontation and the ass kicking I'm sure to receive for sniffing around his daughter. I keep my limbs loose, my eyes focused, and wait for him to cut to the chase.

"You doing okay?" Christ. Now I feel like the asshole of all assholes. Here I am, worrying about him knowing about me and his daughter, and he's asking about me.

"Yeah, a lot better. Sorry about that." He knows I take time off every year on their anniversary to be by myself. This year, it hit harder. My parents being gone for twenty years, the memorial being donated in their name after the property was bought out from underneath them, it was the perfect fucking storm, and it hit me right at the worst possible time.

"Nothing to be sorry about, Fletch. They were damn good people, didn't deserve what happened to them, and you boys didn't either. Plus, I think we all know you could leave for a month without worrying about touching all your accrued paid time off."

"I don't think taking a month off would be a good idea. There's only so many planes a man can jump out of or places to explore until he's ready to be home." Long weekend trips are the key for me to refuel. Of course, now I'm thinking about taking Delilah with me and what she'd think about some of my explorations. One thing is for sure: I wouldn't mind taking her somewhere tropical, a place that has a waterfall, and seeing her in nothing but a bathing suit.

"Probably not, but you take whatever time you need. Though, I can't say your cases would be too happy about the lack of your presence." He gestures toward the stack.

"Yeah, I'd definitely say so." The cases I'm working on aren't anything that demanded attention, mostly follow-ups, court dates, and filing of paperwork. Someone would pitch in if it was dire, or I'd have had Wyatt bring them out to me.

"Well, I'm off. I've got a meeting. Glad you're back." Taylor claps me on my shoulder before he heads toward Susan. The routine is as follows: he makes sure everyone has what they need, tells Susan where he's going and when he expects he'll be back. The man is a creature of habit. It's a good thing we live in a small town with not a lot of crime, or he'd be prime picking for someone on the wrong side of the law.

Chapter 7
Delilah

"Done." The last of my work is completed for the day, and it's still early in the afternoon. Even though I started later than usual, after I walked Fletch out to his truck and said goodbye, watching as he drove off until all I saw were his taillights. Afterwards, it was time for me to get dressed, clean up his place a little, and then head home. I didn't have to make his bed, clean up our dishes, or pick up the discarded item off the floors. In fact, he didn't ask, but I wanted to do something for him, and it's not like it took me a whole lot of time either. Once everything was done, I locked his front door with my key and headed home in yesterday's clothes. The good thing with this apartment is the attached garage. No one had to see me do the walk of shame. I'm not ashamed, though, so the joke would be on whoever felt the need to run their mouth. Sure, it'd be fun to explain to my mother and father. Still, it's not a big deal. Even if the conversation went a little something like this.

"Hi, honey, the tenant next door called and said you never came home last night. I hope everything is okay." That would be Mom's extent. Dad, on the other hand, would go, *"Why weren't you home last night? Did you have car trouble? Did you go home with someone? Tell me who it is."* Mom is soft to Dad's hardness. That's the cop in him, I suppose, and while I love them both, I'm a lot closer to my mom than my dad. A hazard of his job, working weird hours, and when he was home, Dad would still work. The phone never stopped, and cases never slept. Neither did he. I remember waking up for school, and he'd be sitting at the kitchen table, a mug of coffee with a carafe sitting on a hot mitt. There would be times Dad never went to sleep because he worked through the entire night. I wouldn't know, and he wouldn't tell me if I asked. All I know is he'd take a break to make breakfast for the two of us. It was our time together, but because of the time constraint, it still wasn't enough. As an adult looking back, I know he was doing the best he could. Still, twenty minutes a day wasn't enough for a girl to unload all of her daily woes and drama on her dad. When we were just about done with breakfast, Mom would come out of the bedroom, he'd have her cup of coffee ready and her

plate made up in the microwave. She'd take me to school, come back home, then she'd eat breakfast. Seriously, Mom never ate first thing in the morning, whereas Dad and I are ready to eat the second our feet hit the floor. Well now, for Dad that is.

I push back from my makeshift workspace in my apartment, ready to be done with sitting for the day. The folding card table and chair aren't the most comfortable, but it works for the time being. My place is a work in progress. There are still a lot of items I need to purchase. Mom offered to go shopping with me, a pastime we both enjoy, except I wasn't ready to junk up the place for the sake of going on a shopping spree. This is, for all intents and purposes, my first big girl place. My apartment before this one was more like a haphazardly thrown together hot mess express.

My back, neck, and even my ass hurt from sitting in one position for too long. The bath I took after coming home this morning is no longer helping. The slight twinge of pain when I move my legs reminds me of the way Fletcher took me.

"I guess it's time to eat something." My stomach grumbles. I haven't eaten since earlier this morning, and the energy from that bagel is long gone. I'm still in what I like to call my work clothes—a black fitted scoop neck tee sans bra because why bother if I'm not on a live video call with a potential client. A pair of old gray sweatpants from my early days in college and ankle socks. I also keep a jacket nearby in case the air conditioning kicks on. There's nothing worse than being on a computer for hours and freezing to death.

I weigh out my options: get dressed and go to the grocery store or get dressed and see if my best friend, Madelyn, has time to meet up. I pick up my phone, face recognition unlocking it, and got to my contacts. She's the third one down on my favorites list, and my thumb presses her name on the screen. I place the call on speakerphone. It rings a couple of times, giving me ample opportunity to pick up my coffee mug, the various pens, pencils, and notepads I use to scribble my notes on.

"Well, if this isn't a pleasant surprise," Madelyn greets me.

"Wanna meet up for some shopping and pizza?"

Tacos and margaritas sound like a good idea, except then I'd have to drive home, which means limiting myself to one. My best friend living in Peach Springs is the absolute best thing ever. We lived in a dorm room our freshman year, then transferred to an apartment. After graduation, we drifted apart physically to start our lives, yet we talked every single day. A call, a text, a FaceTime call, it never failed that we'd gab on the phone for hours and hours at a time. I hung back, only really visited during holidays and breaks, choosing to stay in college longer than most would. I'm an overachiever, what can I say?

"That's a dumb question. When and where?" This is why I love Madelyn—she's up for anything. Now that she's with Asher and isn't working her fingers to the bone, it's even better.

"The Feather Your Nest, of course." Our town may be small, but we have a lot to do here—vintage shopping, boutiques, nature parks, restaurants, and there's even a bar. "Followed by Peach Pie?" I could really go for a buffalo chicken pizza and a Cesar salad. Yes, I'm the weirdo who eats vegetables with greasy carbohydrate meals. Sue me; it's called balance.

"I'm in," Madelyn replies. I look down at my wardrobe of choice and run my fingers through my hair. It's a knotted mess, and it looks like I'll be keeping it up for the time being.

"Sounds good to me."

"I'll be there in thirty. Can you be ready in that time frame?" she teases me. Yes, it takes me awhile to get ready. Blame it on my penchant for getting sidetracked. I'll start getting dressed, move into the kitchen, wash dishes, go back to getting ready in the way of makeup, then repeat the process, only this time, it'll be another mundane task like making my bed. Finally, after a lot longer than I'd care to admit, I'm ready.

"Umm, maybe?" I reply in more of a question.

"Well, I guess it doesn't matter how long you take. Asher is working, and I have the afternoon free.

Which, by the way, how are you managing to sneak away today?" *Don't think about it, Delilah, do not think about it,* I tell myself over and over again. It's not what you think. I will wholeheartedly spill my guts the minute we are alone and no one else is around. What I'm thinking about has butterflies swirling around in my stomach. It's the potential at seeing Fletcher while I'm in town.

"I'm starving, on the verge of gnawing my arm off and tempted to wear what I have on. Plus, I managed to work for five hours straight without any interruptions." My headphones were in, and I was jamming out to my moody playlist.

"Well, then, I guess we'll find out if you can actually meet me in thirty minutes. In case you didn't know already, I love you, ratty clothes and all." Madelyn laughs.

"Very funny." I laugh and hit the end button. I'm about to make my best friend eat her words.

Chapter 8
Fletch

I'd recognize her car anywhere. Pizza wasn't on my radar after my shift, but it sure as hell is now. I was going to hit up Peaches, the local diner in town, but veered off away from my path I saw Delilah's bright red coupé parked out front of Peach Pie. I was parked and out of my truck faster than I cared to admit. Keeping this shit quiet is going to be harder than I initially thought. My eyes lock on Delilah's back, and when I see she's with my brother Asher's woman, Madelyn, I walk toward the two of them.

"Hey, Fletch," Madelyn greets before I reach the table. Delilah looks over her shoulder and stares right at me. Yep, this shit isn't going to last. Either I'm going to have to buck the fuck up and be a man, or Chief Taylor is going to find out before we're ready.

"Hi, Madelyn, Delilah." The woman who's got me all kinds of screwed up smiles sweetly at me.

"Hey, Fletcher." Her soft voice hits me in the gut and dick.

"I was just heading out. I'll ask Asher about you borrowing his truck. I'm sure he'll tell me no and do it himself instead." Madelyn stands up from her seat, puts a twenty-dollar bill down, and moves toward Delilah.

"Thanks, I appreciate it. See you soon." The girls hug, and I wait patiently while they finish up their silent conversation. There are a bunch of head nods, a wink comes from Delilah, and Madelyn laughs. The whole time, I'm an outsider looking in. It's fucking amazing to watch unfold.

"Later," Madelyn says, nodding to me before walking away.

"What was that all about?" I ask, taking my seat across from Delilah. She cocks her head to the side. I'm not sure if it's because I'm showing my hand by sitting with her in public or about the conversation involving using my brother's truck for my damn woman.

"Care to elaborate?" Delilah follows up with a question of her own.

"Never been around two girls who are friends much; had brothers growing up. I'm not interested in what the two of you said without saying anything. What furniture do you need moved, and why would you go to Asher instead of me?" I rest my forearms on the table in front of us. Madelyn may have been done eating, but it looks like Delilah barely made a dent. She shrugs her shoulder and pushes her food toward me. "Delilah," I push her to respond.

"I'm full. I was starving when we got here, we ordered appetizers, and I thought I needed to follow it up with a medium pizza and a medium salad. Please, help me finish it. As for the furniture, Mad's offered."

"Damn, me too. I'll pick up your furniture and deliver it. I'm off shift for the day. I doubt it'll fit in the squad car. Won't take me long to head home, switch out vehicles, then get it loaded up. What did you get?" I take a bite of her pizza. I'd usually be a bit pickier, wanting the kind with red sauce, a shit ton of meat, and a healthy dose of garlic crust.

"Pretty bold, don't you think? Sitting with me in public, offering to help deliver furniture to my place. I'm not sure it's a good idea, Fletch." Her lips wrap around her straw, and I already know tonight is going to end with them wrapped around my cock. This time, I'll come down her throat, and she'll suck me down, all the way to the back of her throat. I shift in my seat as my length thickens in my jeans. Walking out of here could pose a problem.

"What's the harm in helping out the Chief's daughter?" I'm the biggest dick there is, asking her to keep this charade up while going behind my boss' back.

"I'll call my dad and let him know. Otherwise, some damn neighbor will be running to their phone." I shake my head, lips tipping up in a smile. Good ole' small town living. It never bothered me much before, but now that I've got something to lose, it's not making me feel warm and cozy.

"Alright, will you take payment from me of some kind?"

"Nope, don't even think about it." The waitress comes up to our table.

"Can I get y'all anything?" she asks.

"A Coke to go and the check." There's no sense in beating around the bush, plus it looks like Delilah has something to say.

"Sure thing. I'll be right back with both." I wait until she is gone. The rest of the place isn't very busy, so when Delilah moves closer, forearms on the table, her full tits on full display from the V of her shirt, I do the only thing there is to do: I move closer.

"Then I guess I'll have to repay you in the form of orgasms," she whispers with a rasp, reminiscent of how she says my name when I'm fucking my cock into her tight cunt. There goes us leaving any time soon. The thought of her and orgasms, her mouth on my cock, her riding me until she comes, me tossing her on her back and fucking her into oblivion, it all plays like a reel on repeat in my head. My cock goes from semi to hard like a car goes from zero to sixty in under five damn seconds.

"You're damn right you will. Figure out whose place we'll be at tonight, Delilah. I'm not going another night without hearing you moan my name, having a taste of you on my lips, and feeling you come around my cock," I announce, seeing the waitress making her way back from the corner of my eye. Delilah's eyes are blazing with need, and she nods her head once before following my lead.

"Tonight," she mouths. Fuck, yeah, I'm more than ready to wrap this up, pick up whatever the hell she bought, get it set up, and maybe it'll be big enough for her to lie across while I fuck my woman.

Chapter 9
Delilah

"Holy shit, umm... maybe I should have brought a measuring tape." I'm standing near my open garage door, watching as Fletcher backs into my driveway. My apartment is more like a condo, and I was lucky a unit became available when it did. Sometimes, my spur-of-the-moment plans backfire on me in the worst way possible. I was down to the wire, the lease on my last apartment was ending soon, and my job trying to kill me off didn't help either. So, I made a couple of phone calls to line this place up, and once it was secured, I called my parents. Dad about hit the fan when I laid everything out. He is not a man who likes change, especially when it comes to his only daughter. Which is why sneaking around with Fletcher is good and bad. The fallout, when it comes, will be of epic proportions, but it'll be worth it. You can't convince me any differently. I do worry about Fletch and what it'll mean for his job. I've done some reading online about the process of firing a deputy sergeant when you're the chief. It would be hard for my father to do without a very long process involved. That doesn't mean he couldn't make his life hell for the duration. Which is why we have to be on the same page, because I know my dad. This won't be easy for him to digest. He'll have no problem lashing out, and his tongue can be venom laced.

Fletch puts the truck in park, opens the driver's door, steps out of the truck, and my clit throbs. He's changed since we parted ways at the pizza place. The one thing about not letting anyone know we're together is there are no public goodbyes.

No kiss.

No hugs.

Not even the barest of touches with the tips of our fingers.

My eyes start at the bottom and work their way up. He's still in the same jeans and boots, but his shirt is no longer the starched uniform. Instead, Fletch is wearing a black top with a The Wild Brothers Peach Farm logo. His arms are on full display—one is a full sleeve of tattoos, from shoulder to his knuckles, while the other isn't covered nearly as much, focusing more on his bicep. Still, I can see the design dipping below his shirt sleeve.

"My eyes are up here, Delilah," he states, but I don't give him my full attention. Yet. His muscles flex, and I'm lost in watching as they do when he reaches for the door to shut it. Seriously, this man does things to me that I have never felt before. He takes a step closer, and finally, I avert my gaze to him. "Woman, I can't do shit with us out in the open, and with the way you're looking at me, I'm not going to last another ten seconds."

I move closer, my hand reaching out before I pull it back to my side. Yep, this is one of those moments I'm going to hate having to hide. *Get your shit together, Delilah Taylor.* The faster we get the desk inside, the sooner we can be alone.

"Okay. Well, I think we may have a problem." I blink, trying to change the subject instead of imagining what his lips would feel like pressed against mine. Yes, we kissed when he left this morning, but that was hours upon hours ago.

"Yeah, I'm seeing that." I'm not sure if he's talking about us keeping our distance or how we're going to get the massive desk into my apartment.

"I'll help you," I offer. Fletch's hand goes to the side of the truck, gripping it so tight his knuckles are turning white.

"Oh, you fucking will, Delilah." He takes a deep breath, almost like he's scenting the air. Can he smell me from eight feet away? "Later," he follows up.

I swallow, a lump forming in the back of my throat as I think about what will happen when we're alone. "Okay."

He takes another deep breath. "I didn't realize you had a two-story, or the size of the desk. There's no way in hell you can help me lift this without hurting yourself. Asher couldn't get away from the farm. Beau could, so he should be pulling up any minute. You wanna show me where we're placing this?"

"I'm not sure if I should be offended or flattered," I reply. Besides, it was me who packed up every box, rented a small moving truck, then loaded and offloaded everything on my own before a certain male showed up. That person would be my father. He was pissed at the situation, told me to sit my ass down or unpack the house. He took over, much like he tends to do when the occasion warrants it.

"Delilah, the damn thing weighs nearly three hundred pounds. The guy helping me load it up struggled. The last thing I want is for us to move it and the damn thing to drop on you." Okay, filing this away for future reference, bring a measuring tape and ask how heavy the piece is before purchasing any more furniture.

"Oh, well, when you put it like that. Also, it's not going upstairs. My office is downstairs. The upstairs only has my bedroom." Fletch lets go of the big black truck and walks toward me with a purpose. I take a step back, knowing what will happen. He'll be screwed, and the last thing I want to do is ruin his career.

"Lead the way, Delilah." His voice deepens, taking on a throaty tone. I'm well aware what will happen the minute we walk through my front door. I turn around. His wish is my command. So, what if I put a little bit more into my normal gait? My shoulders no longer slouch, and there's a bit of an arch to my back and a little sway to my hips. The clothes I put on to meet up with Madelyn were immediately discarded when I came home. My sundresses are comfortable, but the jeans I put on were restricting, and the fast cleanup that needed to be done before Fletch got here meant a quick change of clothes. I was back in my work clothes of sweats and tee, and yes, my bra is off, too.

"Woman." Fletch catches up to me as we round the corner to the semi-private walkway leading to the front door. I can feel the heat of his body, and when he wraps his arm around my waist, my back meets his front.

"Fletcher." I move my head when I feel the ghost of his lips trail along the column of my neck.

"A few more steps, then I'll give you my mouth." My mind conjures up exactly where he'll use it. Will it be pressed against my own, will he strip me out of my clothes to suck on my nipples, or will he drop to his knees? I can imagine him lifting my thigh, placing it over his shoulder, and eating me like I'm his last meal.

"Jesus," I breathe out. We take the steps together. My hand wraps around the handle, attempting to turn the damn knob. Fletcher doesn't make this any easier when he sucks on my skin, pulling it into his mouth. My eyes shudder closed, and my chest heaves with each sensation his lips, his tongue, and the way he breathes make me feel. Goose bumps consume my body. I'm a lost cause. There's no way I'll be able to do what we both need and want now. Fletch's hand covers mine, and he twists the handle, opening the door, then walks us inside, his legs on the outside of mine.

"Mouth." I'm spun around, the door is kicked shut, and Fletcher doesn't kiss me; that's too small of a word for what he's doing to me. He's consuming me, mind, body, and soul.

Chapter 10
Fletch

"Sucks we can't do this at your place." We had a moment in her place, my mouth on hers, Delilah's body melting into mine. Of course, I had to cut it short. Beau is nothing if not punctual, considering he had shit of his own to do. I knew when he got there, it was time to get to work. His heavy footsteps told me to cut it short. Delilah was none too thrilled, and when we pulled apart, neither was I. There was a reason for it, too. Cheeks red, nipples tight, and I could smell her arousal. My brother coming over to help, but also at the thought he could see my woman like this, did not make me happy. In fact, I was ready to demand she put a jacket on. Delilah has an issue with wearing bras, not that I blame her, seeing as I'm reaping the rewards whenever I'm around. She must have been reading my mind. At the first knock on her door, she reached for a jacket. I'd have said something, but I would have come off as a callous asshole. She saved me from showing my ass.

"Yeah, well, your truck is massive. Besides that, I wouldn't put it past my dad to do a drive-by on his way home. A habit I seemed to have picked up from him." My truck isn't even that big. A black Chevrolet 2500 isn't big when you grew up on a farm. There are times you have to pull a trailer, and you don't want to get stuck in the wet Georgia clay. I lift my head off the pillow. She's got hers tilted in upward on my chest. That bit of information has my attention. Delilah always does, but now I want to know exactly what she's talking about.

"Why would you be driving by?" I ask. We're on the couch. I'm flat on my back, and she's wedged between my body and the back of the couch. We once again didn't make it to my bed for our first round. This time, I bent her over the back of the couch, and when we were finished, we landed here. Her legs were like jelly, and my own weren't much better. Now she's wrapped around my body, my fingers massaging the nape of her neck. I've got her leg hitched over mine, and there's a mess between her legs leaking on me. It's fucking hot as hell how she doesn't seem to mind, and I damn sure don't.

"Because I knew, Fletcher. I knew that one time with you would never be enough. I didn't have your number, you know. I couldn't necessarily ask my dad, so I drove by the station waiting to see if your police car was in the parking lot so I could thank you. Obviously, you weren't there, and I finally asked Dad where you were. He told me. A quick phone call to my mom, and you know the rest." The look on her face is priceless. She's proud of herself. Damn, so am I. Delilah Taylor, when she wants something, she goes after it. I'm not even going to talk about how I was too much of a dumbass not to do similar. I should have known there was no denying the attraction.

"Thank fuck you did. My head was so screwed up and stuck up my own ass. I can't say I would have done similar." She scoots up, leaving a trail of our combined cum, a slight hiss leaving her lips. "You sore, baby?" I ask.

"What can I say? You're one of a kind, Fletcher Wild. And to answer your question, I could use another good soak in the tub. I'm not sure I've recovered from last night and, well, you're really big." She traces the tattoo on my rib cage.

"Fuck, yeah, I am." I don't tack on that she's small. Her cunt probably won't ever get used to my dick, it sure as hell hasn't so far. I've taken Delilah hard, taken her slow, had my fingers in her pussy, and she's clamping down on me before she's close to coming.

"And now I've stroked your ego." Her laugh is a balm to my damn soul.

"You'll be stroking something else, you keep touching me." Her fingers stop their ministrations for a second, telling me she likes that idea as much as my dick does.

"Promise? You still haven't let me taste you completely." Speaking of dicks, he perks right the fuck up.

"Later, you can sit on my face, and while I eat you, you can suck me dry." I'm about to sit up and carry her to the bathroom. I've got a bath, some Epsom salt, and plenty of hot water for her to soak in. There've been times I've had to pull my weight at the peach farm. Days on end of work when I'm not scheduled for duty take their toll on your body when you're not used to that kind of manual labor day in and day out.

"Don't you dare take it back. Every time my lips so much as wrap around your cock, you find a reason to move me off you. One day, I'm going to wake you up while I suck your cock, then you won't have an excuse." Damn, she's going all out.

"Anytime you wanna do that, Delilah, I'm fucking game. Come on, let's get you in the bath."

"Wait, I'm not ready to get up yet. I'm comfortable here." The light jostling of sliding out from beneath her stops. I resettle how we were and hold her close to me.

"Then we'll stay here until you're ready for a

bath." Whatever Delilah wants is whatever Delilah will get.

"Will you take one with me?" There's a hope in her tone. Maybe she doesn't think I'd get in the tub with her. A lesser man may not, but I will.

"Yep. Any chance to have you wet, naked, and in my arms, I'm going to take it."

"Fletcher." She uses her feet on my calf to push her face closer to mine, and I know where this is going.

"I take your mouth, we won't get in the bath, and you'll end up so sore there'll be no sex for a few days. Neither of us wants that. I don't want you sore either."

"Fine, I won't kiss you, then." She goes back to tracing my tattoo. "You know, I've wanted a tattoo for a really long time but haven't pulled the trigger." I'm surprised by that, and she must realize it by the way she looks at my arched eyebrow. "It's a want, but I'm not sure what I want, you know?" Each of my tattoos has a meaning. The clock on my sleeve is my parents' time of death, the numbers on my knuckles are the year the peach tree farm was established, the wings on my other arm are reminiscent of my parents as well. Angels in the sky, so to speak.

"Whenever you figure out what you want, I'll take you. My guy is in Wyoming. Lawson, my buddy, knows the guy, and all of them have their work done there as well. Only guy I'd trust with my skin." I won't be able to get away from work for a little while. The next time I do, it'll be to take Delilah up to Wyoming with me. Let her meet the other people I call family.

"I'd like that. I've got a couple of ideas." She takes my hand and brings it to the underside of her tit. "I'm thinking one right here to start out." My pointer finger traces her flesh, thumb sweeping over her pebbled nipple.

"Fuck." The second it's healed, my tongue will be tracing whatever design she chooses.

"I think we should go take that bath now. If not, I'm going to beg you to take me, and sitting in an office chair for work isn't going to help the soreness," she all but purrs. She's right. Damn, do I hate the fact. I want nothing more than to wrap my mouth around her nipple and suck it into my mouth.

"You got it." I stand up before she has a chance to change her mind. My cock is hard as it is, and even with our combined cum drying between her legs, I felt her heated flesh. She'd try to take me again, and I'd be the selfish dick to take from her, too.

Chapter 11
Delilah

Two days in, and we've already created a routine. I spend the night at Fletcher's, make us breakfast, watch him get dressed while I do the same, and we walk out the door together. When Fletch saw me repack my overnight bag, he grumbled, told me to bring enough over for a few days as well as any toiletries I'd need here. Apparently, he noticed me not using his shampoo. The lack of conditioner in his bathroom was all I needed to know to wash my hair at my apartment. My hair has a natural wave to it, which would mean nothing but frizz city. Mom got the lustrous curls, Dad has stick straight hair, and I got the in-between, but there are some days when the humidity isn't crazy that the wave is super defined.

I'm tapping away at my computer after coming home. I turned on the coffee pot to have another cup or three. The late couple of nights are starting to catch up with me. Sleep is my best friend, literally and figuratively. Fletcher Wild may not know this about me yet, but without at least seven hours of sleep at night, well, it's going to make for a very grumpy Delilah soon. At this rate, after work, I may have to crawl into bed to take a nap.

I'm attempting to get comfortable in my makeshift office chair, a task that is nearly impossible. My desk may be amazing with all kinds of drawers to put away my plethora of shit I like out while working on accounts, taxes, and payroll, but the same can't be said for my chair. It's one of those folding metal types. Madelyn and I looked high and low for a chair to go with the desk while at the vintage store, but needless to say, we came up short. I'm more than likely going to have to order one from a big box store, and that doesn't make me very happy, unless they have a style that will go with what I've found.

I have my headphones on and am jamming out to my moody playlist, completely in the zone, when I damn near have a heart attack. Out of the corner of my eye, I see a movement. I whip my over-the-ear noise cancelling headphones off. "Mom! Jesus, you scared the piss out of me." She's standing there with a couple of bags in one hand, the other hand over her chest.

"Well, you gave me a heart attack, so I'd say we're even. Though, you may want to go change your pants." And she may be right about that. There are two people who have a key to my place: my mom and now Fletcher. I may need to set some ground rules with Marigold Taylor. Had this been yesterday, well, things could have played out differently.

"You're not wrong about that. This is a pleasant surprise, Mom. Did you bring me goodies?" There was a time I would come home from college and shop their pantry for the good snacks. While I got a scholarship and worked as a teacher's aid, there wasn't a lot for extras. Dad wasn't the chief at the time I left. Mom was only working part-time once I was in middle school, so it's not like they were rolling in the dough. Which meant the extras were few and far between. I'd stock up on toilet paper, body wash, the good snacks, and Mom would always leave a bag by the front door with tampons and pads.

"The usual." She plops the bags on the edge of my desk. "This is sweet. Vintage shop?" My love for thrifting and antiquing came from the woman in front of me. We'd go on days when it was too hot to be outside. Sometimes, we'd buy a new-to-us item, but most of the time we didn't. On those days, we'd stop and get ice cream as a small treat.

"Of course." The desk is probably four foot wide by six feet long, there are drawers on both sides, and it has vintage brass pull handles. It was the beautiful honey colored wood and the feet that stole my attention. Beneath the three drawers on each side are spindle style legs and a floating shelf, and the feet are just as beautiful—they're carved and adorned with metal castor wheels. It was also a steal, and I was ready to run to make the purchase in case someone else snatched it up before me.

"Looks like it's British, too." Mom drags her hand along the top.

"I think it may be. There's a stamp on it, but I couldn't really decipher it. All I know is she's a beast and is really heavy." I stand up, needing to stretch and obviously start back up my yoga. Since I've moved back home, the only exercise I have been doing is between the sheets.

"Most vintages are. How'd you get it home?" There's no reason to lie. It's not a secret like my relationship.

"Fletcher and Beau. I was at the pizza place with Madelyn when Fletcher walked in and heard Mads offer Asher's truck. He suggested his truck at home would work, so Fletch picked it up and Beau helped." I shrug my shoulders, trying to come off nonchalantly.

"Your dad would have helped. I know you've done it on your own for years now, but we're here, too." Mom is right. I'm not one to ask for help. It's a problem of mine.

"I'm not sure it would have fit in Dad's patrol vehicle. It barely fit in Fletch's truck. I guess something came up, both the Wild brothers showed up, made it look like a cake walk, and left. Though I'm probably going to need to bake more cookies. He mentioned they were all gone, and now that he helped me yet again, it'll be time to bake another batch, plus whatever Beau's favorite are. You don't happen to know his, do you?"

"Take a breath, Delilah. You're probably right on the desk. Plus, your father had a meeting and wouldn't have been able to help. I have no idea what Beau likes, but I'm sure Fletcher will share his chocolate chip cookies." Fletch barely shared the cookies I baked for him with me. I highly doubt he'll share with Beau. He does not like to share, so I guess I'll have to figure something else out.

"True, that's settled. A triple batch of cookies it is. You want to sit in the living room? My office still has a long way to go." I grab the bags off the desk and wait for her to head toward the open doorway. My apartment has a living room, kitchen, and then what I'm using as an office. They advertised it as a game room. There's no closet, and it can't be classified as a bedroom without it. That's okay because the only person who would need to stay would be Madelyn. Asher would never allow her to spend the night now that they're rock solid. Fletcher is in bed with me or vice versa, and the double glass doors add a brightness to the office I never knew I'd appreciate.

"Sure, honey." I'm hoping I've done a good enough job to keep things under wraps. "I will say this, you're positively glowing."

"What do you mean, glowing?" I feel my cheeks and neck, wondering if I'm blushing. If that's the case, I'm screwed.

"You know, the glow women have when they're pregnant or in love." My stomach sinks to my feet.

"I'm not pregnant, and I'm definitely not in love." I cross my fingers. Lying to my mom is a new territory for me.

"Maybe it's being home that's doing it to you. The fresh air, unlike the polluted air in the city." Or it could be the multiple orgasms I'm receiving every night.

"Could be. Coffee? I'm afraid lunch will have to be sandwiches, chips, and fruit." My fridge has the bare essentials. I still need to hit the grocery store for my weekly meal prep and planning. Maybe when Mom heads out, I'll get some shopping done and figure out dinner at Fletch's.

"Yes on the coffee, no for lunch." She shakes her head yet smiles softly. "I'm meeting your father at Peach Pie. Care to join us?"

"I probably would, but I ate there yesterday. I think between Mads and me, we devoured two appetizers, most of our pizzas, and I barely touched my salad. People would probably talk if I ate there two days in a row with how I chowed down."

"Must be nice to have your dad's metabolism. You, my sweet daughter, got all the good genes." She's right. I do gain weight like others, though it's only when I'm sedentary. Working out daily helps combat that. Dad, on the other hand, has a penchant for beer and sports a slight paunch because of the hops he enjoys. As for me, my job requires a lot of sitting, which means food will go to my hips and ass if I'm not careful.

"You're perfect the way you are. Come on, let's have that coffee before Dad steals my mother away from me." I drop the bags on the kitchen counter, then go through the motions of getting Mom a mug down from my cabinet.

"Delilah Ann Taylor, get out of the way." I tried to close the door as quickly as possible. When I moved in, everything was shoved in a haphazard manner. I've yet to get around to organizing, and my mother can't handle it.

"Fine, I suppose," I tease because I'd love nothing more than for her to help me get my kitchen in better shape than it currently is.

"I'm calling your father. He can bring lunch over for all of us. This is going to take a while." Mom pulls her sleeves up and starts on cleaning up what she deems a travesty. Meanwhile, I head back to my office to call my dad. Seems I'm going to have pizza two days in a row. You won't hear me complaining.

Chapter 12
Fletch

"Fletcher, there's been a call for a welfare check. Are you able to check it out on your way out?" Susan asks when I'm about to say my goodbyes for the day. The past two days, I've been stuck to my desk. I've wrapped up case after case, signing my name, following up, and I can finally see the light at the end of the tunnel.

"Sure can. Paper or on the computer?" I ask.

"Computer. Chief Taylor said it's time to get with this century." For the most part, she'll write up a report and hand it to me, but on the rare occurrences, she'll put it in the system. Susan looks around and over her shoulder. "Truth be told, I think the big guy came down on him. Computers are so much easier, and then there's no need for all these files sitting around." The man has been set in his ways for years now, used to doing things his own way. But when the mayor and town officials tell you to get with the program, you don't have much of a choice.

"That'll put him in one hell of a mood." The paper trail is a pain in the dick and a fuck of a lot easier to lose. Especially when your desk is full of them. "Maybe digital signatures will be next." I wink at Susan. She's been grumbling about how it'd make things a hell of a lot easier if she didn't have to print out documents for us all to sign.

"We can only hope. I'm not holding my breath, though." The phone on her desk rings, but she ignores it for a second, minus her hand being on the receiver, and says, "Keep me posted, alright? The caller seemed upset."

"You got it." I tap my knuckles on her desk before heading out the door. It's time for me to get this show on the road.

"Thank you, Fletcher." I don't get to respond. She answers her phone and is back to business. My feet carry me to the door. With Susan being at the station alone, I'll make sure to lock the door when I leave. Peach Springs is nothing like where I used to work, a big city where crime was sky high, and I worked undercover on drug cases. I had my fill, tired of being gone for weeks on end, unable to talk to my family and friends. Of course, I'd get the itch to head out, jump from a plane, zip line in the clouds, or rock climb in the desert.

"Shit," I whisper under my breath as I open and close the door, locking it after me. Ever since Delilah has been in my life, I've felt more settled than I ever have. There's been no need to go seek the next adrenaline rush. Even when I tucked tail and ran back to Wyoming to get away from the temptation that is Delilah Taylor, I wasn't out riding a bull or bucking bronc like I once would have. My woman has me settling down and changing my ways. The kicker of it all is, there would be a time in my life when the thought alone would have me running for the hills. Now I'm the one ready to run toward Delilah. Damn, I'm going to be eating my words to my brothers and definitely to my buddy Lawson. I shake my head. It's time get this show on the road. The sooner I take care of this call, the faster I can get home to my woman.

--

After a fifteen-minute drive, I turn onto the street Susan put in the system. The neighborhood is quiet. There's an older couple sitting in folding chairs underneath the tree in their front yard. I give them a two-finger wave, keeping my eyes peeled for where I'm going. Another neighbor is at the mailbox and waves me down. I'm going to go out on a limb and say this might be the person who made the call, and things must not be too bad if he's out here without a care and flagging me down. I slow to a stop, roll my window down, and say, "Hello, sir."

"Hey, there, are you coming here because of all the traffic coming and going lately?" My interest is piqued. I wouldn't have suspected a neighborhood with a one-way street having traffic.

"Not particularly, but I'll see what I can do. When you say traffic, what time of day and night?"

"At night. They like to use it like a runway, flying down the block, the noisier, the better. Enough to wake a man up from his sleep," the gentleman states. I stay quiet. Usually, the best way to get the information you want is by waiting and letting the other person get everything out of their system. "I'm not sure if drugs are involved, if they're night owls or what. I do know the house is a rental, there are more men than women, and there's also a little girl. She must be about three or four. We all watch out for one another around here and, well, the little girl ran into the street one evening when I was coming in from dinner. A truck was heading right for her. Faster than I thought these old bones could take me, I got her out of the way." He shakes his head. While this isn't a crime, accidents happen, but if it's continuously happening, well, it could be a case of neglect.

"Anyways, I suspect you're here because of all the complaints. I'll let you be, just wanted to give you my two cents."

"I appreciate that and will look into it," I reply.

"Thanks." He nods, backs away from my vehicle, and I continue my way to the house in question. I hit the button on my two-way. "Sergeant Wild, I'm at the residence," I radio into dispatch, waiting for a response before I step out of my car. The house in question looks like it's one of those landlord specials, a quick flip to make a buck, and if what the older gentleman was saying is true, then a rental is easy money.

"10-4," dispatch responds on the other end. I step out of my car and pocket my keys. I resituate my bulletproof vest. The damn thing likes to sit up high when you're sitting down. While we're pretty relaxed at the station, not having to wear the standard uniform like most precincts, we're still cautious. Out of habit, my hand lands on my hip where the police-issued Glock 43 is in its holster, safety on but at the ready. On the other side of my belt is a Taser and handcuffs. My badge hangs on a chain around my neck. I walk up the driveway toward the house for the welfare check. When I got in my car, powered up my laptop, and read through the report, it was pretty vague. An individual called the station, stating they hadn't heard from their daughter in a couple of days. They live out of town and weren't able to come down for another two days. The grass is a bit overgrown, there are a couple of trucks that look like they've seen better days, and toys are here and there. A playhouse, a slide, and a wood bench swing hanging from the tree with rope.

I walk up the front steps, sweeping my eyes back and forth. There's no noise coming from inside, but I knock anyways. "Peach Springs police," I announce. I'm not expecting a response. I knock one last time, repeating who's at the door, and still, nothing.

"Dispatch, this is Sergeant Wild," I speak into my two-way again.

"This is dispatch, go ahead."

"There's no answer at the residence." I'll make time tomorrow to either come during my shift or see if Chief Taylor wants me to stick around later in order to come back when someone will be home. Either that, or he can assign another deputy to take over. I know Taylor enough, though; once you take on a call, he likes you to see it through.

I'm walking back down the driveway when a neighbor is out walking her dog, or more like the dog is walking her. A small canine, what most would call an ankle biter, whose bark is a lot bigger than his bite. Still, I don't move until her dog is more secure.

"Batman, that's enough." I watch as she brings him in, slowly, until she's got the miniature Yorkie within reach. The young woman bends down and picks up her wannabe voracious beast. "Sorry about that." She looks over her shoulder. "You won't see any activity at that house until the sun goes down. Unless it's the weekend, then it's party central."

"I'll try back then."

"The mom and little girl are usually out then, too. The weekdays are hit and miss." Makes me wonder if someone from out of town really did call it in or if it was one of the neighbors instead. Either way, a wealth of knowledge has been given to me in the short minutes I've been here, and I'll be sure to document it.

"Thanks, I appreciate it. Have a good day," I tell her, sensing we were at the end of her information dump.

"You're welcome. You too." She puts Batman back on the ground and then turns in the opposite direction of where she was walking before. Yeah, I'd bet twenty bucks a neighbor called this is in. Smart, if you think about it. Even with asking to be anonymous, people in small towns talk, word gets around, and if you don't know these people well enough, who knows what they could do or say. I unlock the doors to my car, hitting the automatic start button once I'm close enough, and while I'd usually stay where I am to write my report, I think I'll do it once I get to the house, where I've got a woman waiting for me at home.

Chapter 13
Fletch

I turn down the long gravel driveway of the farm, seeing Asher and Madelyn up ahead in the golf cart. I could easily be an asshole, hit my lights and sirens to scare the piss out of them. And I would if Madelyn weren't with my oldest brother. I'd like to get home to Delilah. The last thing I need is him trying to whoop my ass for scaring the shit out of Madelyn. It's not like I wouldn't do the exact same thing if Asher did similar to Delilah.

Asher waves me around, and I don't bother stopping to chat. I'll lose track of time, and the text Delilah sent, a picture with her in the kitchen, standing at the stove, a glass of wine in her hand, a soft smile, and I'll just bet she's not wearing a bra beneath her tee, makes me not want to lose a second. Less than a week in her company, and here I am, rushing to get home after work, ready to get inside instead of staying well past quitting time at the station. As soon as I've rounded my brother and Madelyn, I continue my journey until I'm toward the back of the farm. Asher lives in the main house. Beau has a room, too, but I prefer to live on my own, and Asher did a lot for us growing up, shit so did our oldest brother Owen. If anyone deserves the man house it's those two. I'm not sure Owen wants it now that he's out doing his own thing. The fresh scent of peaches blooming comes through the air vent, and while I may not work here full-time like I'm sure our parents would have wanted, I still like having some of the perks of having the family last name, and it's not like I won't pitch in when needed.

    I pull into the paved driveway. Delilah's car is in the garage, where it belongs. My personal truck doesn't fit in it, and my squad car can stay outside for all I care. I make quick work of putting my car in park, turning off the ignition, and unlatching my seatbelt. The longest part of the process is getting my gear inside, particularly my laptop. Every police car has a computer stand included in their car; it can be a pain in the ass to move it in and out of our vehicle. Hopefully, I can do it without Delilah coming out here to greet me before I make it inside. She met me out here yesterday after work, and I'm hoping it's not going to become a tradition like her morning sends offs when I head to the station. It'd be hard as hell to pull a fast one on her if she were to meet me outside today.

"Fuckin' A." I finally get the damn thing loose without my laptop sliding off the stand and hitting the floorboard. Now that it's in my hands, I'm backing out of my SUV, closing the door, and looking at the front porch. Looks like I've got luck on my side, and I'll get to see my woman in the kitchen. I'm annoyed with myself for this taking as long as it has. Hell, I should have been home an hour ago. Susan asking me to go on a call made it to where I'm later than normal. A habit of mine that is slowly changing. Usually I'd work until I was exhausted, now I'm rushing home. I wouldn't usually mind, except now I've got someone to come home to. I may as well name it *Before Delilah* and *After Delilah*. I've gotta say, I like the me *After Delilah* a whole fuck of a lot better. She grounds me in a way that makes me wanna set roots.

"Hey, you're home." I open the front door after rushing up the small walkway from the driveway to the porch. A door that I know is locked when either of us leave the house, yet it was unlocked when I just opened it. Damn, I get the house is way out here; still, I don't like the fact Delilah is here by herself when anyone can waltz in.

"You know how to shoot a gun?" I ask without saying hello back. She's not fazed by my abruptness.

"Yes, I know how to shoot a gun. I have my own,

too, a Smith & Wesson M&P Shield Plus." My cock hardens, thinking about how she'd look with a gun in her hand at a range. Legs shoulder width apart, arms out, the palm of her hand holding the one with her pistol in it. Fuck, yeah, I'd push my luck, too, press my body up against hers, drag my hand up her outer thighs, and in a perfect world, she'd be wearing a sundress. Damn, but I love when she gives me access to her body easily. "Anything else you need to know?"

"Yeah, why the front door was unlocked, and when am I gonna see you shoot?"

Chapter 14
Delilah

I watch as Fletcher Wild closes and locks the front door. The emphasis of him turning the deadbolt echoes through the room. There's an urban legend of sorts that claims we marry our fathers. Well, right now, I can't debunk that statement whatsoever. "I knew you were on your way home. You sent me a message twenty minutes ago. You see, I've got my hands full, well, five minutes ago, before it was time to start working with the dough, I unlocked the door. As for the other part of your question, name the time and place. I'll guarantee you I'm a good shot."

Fletch's eyes heat with need, he sucks in his cheeks, and I watch as his teeth press down onto his plush lower lip. It's a good thing I'm leaning against the counter. Watching him go through his evening routine is hot as hell. I've seen him dress and undress, but I couldn't tell you which is my favorite. I'd say both are equally as hot. A man in uniform is hotter than hot. A man you love in uniform... well, that's off the charts hot.

"Delilah." I avert my gaze from his hands working on his police duty belt. I'm remembering his deft fingers doing wickedly amazing things to me any time he can get his hands on my body.

"Hmm," I respond, licking my lips. Our eyes lock. He's ready to attack me in a way that I'll forget about the dinner I have made and the cookies I'm baking.

"No more leaving the door unlocked when I'm not home. I hope like hell you don't do it at your apartment either." I go start to tell him of course not, I am, after all a cop's daughter, except I'm unable to as Fletch carries on, "I'm sure you can take care of yourself, so don't think I'm doubting you for a minute. It's the other fuckers out there who can hurt you, okay?" He is a natural protective alpha male, and I'm the lucky girl who gets to call him mine. I nod my response. Dad told me when Fletcher settled in at Peach Springs Police Department, he came from a bigger precinct. One where he worked undercover in a unit. Dad didn't elaborate what he did, but I'm beginning to think it had something to do with his time as an undercover agent in the narcotics unit when he was in the city. A shiver runs down my spine. He must have seen a lot and dealt with a lot.

"I can do that, and my apartment is never unlocked when I'm by myself. Even when I'm not, the door is locked by either you, my mom, or Madelyn," I clarify, wanting to reassure him. His body relaxes in what I'm sure is relief. "Please continue," I do a slow perusal of his body, ready to watch him continue stripping down.

"Is that what you'd like, Delilah? You want me to take everything off?" His voice is deep and husky, doing nothing to stop the way my insides quiver for him.

"I can't. I've got to finish making these cookies for you and Beau." I somehow managed to time the chicken casserole dinner being done a few minutes before the cookies were going to start being baked.

"Cookies for who?" Fletcher asks. Gone are his police belt, boots, and hat. He's working his way down the buttons of his shirt, revealing his golden sun-kissed chest. My god. I ignore his question. I'm solely focused on his striptease. "Woman, you gonna answer my question, or do I need to get your attention in another way?"

The clattering of spoons hitting the countertop is jarring. I was using them to form balls for the chocolate chip cookie dough, but my hands drop them and grab the hand towel off to the side to wipe the dampness from the palms of my hands. "For you and Beau. You all helped me with the desk, so I figured I'd repay the favor."

"Turn the oven off, Delilah. Your cookies are mine, not anyone else's," he states as he finishes taking off his shirt, and I'm fumbling to do as he says.

"They're only cookies, Fletcher. I'm not giving him *my* cookie." I've done it now. I've unleashed the beast, and dinner along with the dough will be abandoned for the time being.

"They're your cookies, which mean they're mine. Apparently, you need a reminder of that." He grabs the handcuffs off his belt. My nipples tighten beneath my top, thighs slick with arousal, and there's no cooling off when Fletcher is looking at me like that. The promise in his heated tone, the way his body moves with each step he takes. Slow and calculated.

"Very much so." Only the kitchen island is between us once he makes his way toward me. I'm not sure if I should run toward him or run away. If I run from him, he'll chase after me, which is what spurs me on.

I want to be caught by Fletcher Wild.

I want to be loved by Fletcher Wild.

I want to be consumed by Fletcher Wild.

And I want everything Fletcher Wild is willing to give me.

He must sense that I'm going to bolt, I spin fast on my heels, arms pumping and feet rushing across the kitchen floor. I'm smiling widely. Fletcher is hot on my heels. I'm barely able to look over my shoulder for fear that he'll catch me as soon as I round the island. He's fast, has to be for his job, but I also want this little game to last longer than a millisecond.

"Now you've done it. My handcuffs are going to look damn pretty around your wrists while you're naked on my bed." I stutter in my race. Still, I'm a couple of steps ahead. I'm sure he's giving me a little bit of a head start, and I'm going to use it to my advantage. Two can play this game. I push the straps of my dress down while keeping up my momentum, doing a shimmy to help its way to the floor.

"You have to catch me first," I goad, and no sooner do I make it down the hallway than I feel his arm band around my waist, his hot chest to my back, and his clothed covered cock is wedged between the cheeks of my ass.

"Gotcha, Delilah." He nips at my ear, and I melt into his warmth.

"I gave up pretty easily," I say with a gasp as his hand travels up until he's palming my breast.

"You good with this?" he asks. I'm so lost in euphoria, Fletcher could ask for anything, and I'd more than likely give it to him. I don't answer him fast enough, so he pinches my nipple to get my attention. "Delilah, I'm going to cuff you to the bed, then I'm going to use my mouth on every inch of your body. I'll make you come with my fingers inside your pussy, my lips wrapped around these pretty nipples. I'll work you up again until you're on the edge, then right before you tip over, I'll pull back and slam my cock deep inside you and come with you."

"Yes, please, Fletcher. Please." My knees weaken. I want all of that and more.

"You're in for it now, Delilah." He spins me around, bends at the knees, my stomach going to his shoulder, his hand lands on my ass with a thwack, and I'm being carried down the hall to his bedroom. My hands move to his firm butt, and I squeeze, causing another sharp smack to mirror the slight sting of the other cheek.

"Fletch." I wiggle my legs, trying to alleviate the ache between my thighs. I'm silently praying he quickens his pace, and we can finally get to the part where he makes me come, repeatedly, over and over again.

Chapter 15
Fletch

"What's up, big brother?" Justice says on the second ring. There are only two years between Justice and me. From oldest to youngest, it goes Owen, Asher, me, Justice, Colton, and Beau.

"Calling to check in. Haven't heard from you in a minute." He's been out doing his own thing. A musician who has a hit song and everything. I couldn't be prouder of him, but there's a selfish part of me that would like to see him come home to settle down.

"I'm good, living the good life, you know? How are things your way?" He's hedging, giving me the smallest pieces possible. I get it. We all kind of went our separate ways at times. Shit, it was me who left to go fuck around when I graduated high school, move from place to place until I landed in Wyoming. I met Lawson

Johnson at a bar, things got rowdy when some dumb fucker decided to get handsy with one of the waitresses, and we took action. It also landed us in our own set of silver bracelets until our names were cleared. That's how we became friends and still are to this day.

"Fuck, where do I even begin? I'm in deep, man. Deeper than I've ever been. I'm talking Mom and Dad kind of deep." I can see my life planned out—coming home every night to Delilah like I did last night, although the damn thing would be locked, a ring on her finger, my kid inside her. She'd be in one of her sundresses or sweats with one of her tees. Delilah has an aversion for undergarments once she's home for the day, and I'm hoping she'll always be that way. I'd walk straight to her, take her in my arms, and kiss her until she's breathless. Hell, it wouldn't matter if she was in the kitchen. Delilah could be sitting on the couch, watching one of her sitcoms she enjoys so much, and I'd still do the same damn thing.

"Who's the lucky lady?" Justice asks. I'm in my car on the way to the station, except I'm going to do a drive-by of the house from yesterday. After I made good on my promise, fucking Delilah with my fingers and mouth while she was handcuffed to my bed, only when she boneless, begging for a break, skin slick with perspiration, hair a knotted mess, and flush from head to toe, did I unlock the cuffs. I'd barely rubbed her wrists and shoulders, making sure the circulation was back to normal, when she was attacking me. My cock was more than ready, her pleas about being unable to take much more long gone. Delilah lined her pussy up to my dick and sank down. My mouth went to hers, swallowing down her moans, and she was coming once again, taking me along with her.

"Delilah Taylor, the police chief, my boss', daughter." Justice lets out a low whistle. "That's not all. I'm falling in love with her." I'm not ashamed for what I feel for Delilah. I'm worried about how this is all going to play out more than anything. I may lean more on the wild side, but I'm not a gambler, and our relationship right now is a high stakes game. And Chief Taylor could call all the shots.

"Man, when you grab life by the balls, you go all out. I'm not sure I have any advice, if that's what you're looking for." I wasn't really looking for it. There's none I need, really. We either continue hiding our relationship, or we tear the Band-Aid off in one quick rip. The only problem with that is the fallout I'm sure will come. Neither of us could potentially come out unscathed. Delilah is the one I worry about the most. "I will say this, a love like Mom and Dad's, you'd be stupid not to pursue it."

"That's what we're doing. The sneaking around is going to get hard though. I can only ask the family to keep their mouth shut for so long, and it'd sure as shit be nice to take Delilah out for a date instead of locking us away at my place all the time." She hasn't complained, and neither have I, especially after last night.

"You ask me, being locked away with a pretty woman sounds like a damn good idea." I hear music playing in the background and someone calling Justice's name. Our conversation is going to come to an end. It sounds like he may be at the studio, which means he'll be missing in action until he comes up for air.

"It's not all bad. I'll let you go, but, Justice?" I hear him tell someone to hold up a minute.

"What's that, Fletch?"

"Don't be a stranger. The phone works both ways, you know." I'd have asked him when he's coming home, but I know his schedule is crazy and he will when he can.

"Is this your way of saying you love and miss me?" There's a lightness to his tone.

"Fuck you." I'm going to have to call Owen soon. Surely, the oldest brother in the Wild family will have some kind of advice.

"Fuck you, too."

"Love and miss you, brother." We might joke, but down to the root of us, we all have love for one another.

"Same, gotta go." He hangs up the phone as I'm pulling down the street from yesterday's call. This early in the morning, the whole neighborhood is quiet, the curtains are still drawn, and it looks like everyone is sleeping. I can't say I wouldn't do the same if my hours were a little different. It doesn't take me long to do a slow drive-by of the house. I note there are about five or six vehicles, all trucks, mentally cataloguing them in case they're needed later. I do a quick turnaround in the cul-de-sac, making sure I don't miss any important clues I'll need to document, then go on my way. Once I get back to the station, I'll finish writing up my report, talk to Chief Taylor, and tell him what I found out. Maybe I'll stop by over the weekend, and we can finish getting the welfare check taken care of.

After my quick perusal without any interruptions from neighbors, I leave the street and head toward the station. Lately, with Delilah at the house, I'm not stopping for breakfast or coffee at the local diner. It gives me a few more minutes at home with my woman, and I'm not going to complain about that.

The buzz of my phone alerts me to a text notification. I glance down to see it's Owen. After a quick look shows no one is behind me, I decide to pull over on the side of the road. The fact that Owen is texting me first when I was going to do similar has me shaking my head. It's like fucking *ESP* or some shit.

> Owen: The word of the day is your legs.

> Me: Jesus, do I even want to guess?

> Owen: Let's go home and spread the word.

> Me: Does this shit actually work on women in your bar?

The bubbles start before they disappear again. He's gotta be heading home from his brewery about this time. Usually, I'll wake up to one of these texts; I'll respond while he's asleep and won't hear from him again until I'm about ready to head home.

> Owen: The fucker walked out of the bar with her, so it'd be safe to assume it does. Everything good your way?

> Me: Shocks the fuck out of me. Yeah, may touch base with you after a while.

> Owen: Give me a few hours, and I'll call you. I'm just getting into bed.

> Me: Sounds good.

> Owen: Be safe out there.

I back out of the texts, lock my phone, and put it back in the cup holder. It's time to get to the station and figure out what I'm doing today.

Chapter 16
Delilah

"You're awfully quiet this morning." We've settled into a routine over the past week. My time is split up fifty-fifty—my days are at home and my nights are with Fletcher. This time, I'm sitting on top of the bathroom counter watching as he shaves, mourning the loss of the slight beard he was growing. I knew it wasn't going to last, the beard, not our relationship. It goes against regulation to have a beard too long. The only type of facial hair you can have is a mustache, and Fletch has made it known that he doesn't like them. The good news is, neither do I.

"Not sure how much longer I can do this." I didn't see this coming, not from a mile away. My breakfast sits like lead in my stomach, trying to come up with the right words to say when Fletcher puts any doubts I had to rest. "Get that shit outta your head. This is not me ending things. That was poor wording without any context." He drops the razor in the sink, grabs the towel from the counter, and wipes off his face, coming away clean shaven.

"We can agree on that. I thought my breakfast was about to come back up." I take a deep breath, worry still sitting in the pit of my stomach. Mom never started a heavy discussion with Dad before he went on shift. Yet here I am, ready to poke and prod to get down to the root of whatever is bothering him.

"Fuck, Delilah, I'm sorry. We're not going anywhere, we're rock fucking solid." Fletch moves in front of me, pushing my legs apart to wedge himself between them. "I'm talking about the guilt. It's eating at me."

My eyes look into his, finding the truth behind them, and while I've loved being sequestered away each and every night, he's right. We need to come out and talk to my dad.

"I'm ready whenever you are. We're two consenting adults. This isn't high school, where our hormones are fueling our love for one another. We'll tell him today after your shift at the station." We've kept our relationship under wraps for a few reasons. We were just getting to know one another and wanted to see how deep this was, and my dad is his boss. Hello, alarm bells ringing in every direction possible.

"I want you to be sure. There's a reason I've been

holding back going to your father and laying it all out." Our fingers entwine, and he places our hands on the tops of my thighs. "I don't want to come between you and your father. You get that I don't have my parents, and it hurts like hell. I'd never want that for you, ever." This man, clearly, he's been wrestling with his emotions over this for a while.

"Are you worried he's going to make me choose between you and him?" I ask.

"Yeah, look at you and look at me. I've never once wanted to settle down. I take risks, enjoy the thrill of the chase. Fuck, I wouldn't want you for me if the roles were reversed and you were my daughter. My job, while not being near as dangerous as it once was, shit could happen. I could be taken tomorrow, leaving you behind with a child." His hand disconnects from mine, he places his big palm on my lower abdomen, and continues, "Would you want that for our child?"

My hand cups his jaw, thumb sweeping over his now smooth skin. "I want you, no matter what. If roles were reversed and we were talking about our daughter, yes. I'd want her to know what it's like to live how she wants and love who she wants. Life is too short not to be happy. So, while yes, something could happen, it doesn't mean it will."

"Delilah." He states my name like I'm his reckoning.

"Fletcher."

"You saying you love me, woman?" I'd roll my eyes if this weren't a serious conversation. How could he not see or feel the love I have for him? It's everywhere in everything we do.

"Yes, Fletch, I'm telling you I am completely and utterly in love with you." Regardless of what people may think or say, you can fall in love with someone in a matter of days or weeks. Love doesn't have a time stamp, and your feelings don't need to be validated by anyone who doesn't belong in your relationship. So, while we may have jumped ahead in time from what others have done, it doesn't mean anything less.

"Thank god. I fucking love you, too." His lips land on mine, the palms of his hands cup my cheeks, and my hands encircle his wrists. Fletch takes over the kiss, our tongues tangling with one another. It's full of depth, emotion, and understanding.

Our kiss is filled with love.

He's not trying to dominate me this time; he's giving as much as I am. Exactly how a relationship works. I've had two amazing role models show me what it's like to have what I hope Fletch and I will. He has too, even if his parents were taken away from him and his brothers too soon.

"We're going to finish this, temptress. Later when I get home not like last night. Tonight, it'll be nice and slow. I want you riding my cock and my mouth on you."

"I'm the temptress? Listen, hot stuff, you're the one who makes me this way, but yes, when you get home, I'm going to ride you, and when we come. It'll be with our mouths on one another." I lift up, placing a soft kiss on his lips before wiggling myself off the counter. It seems I've got places to be today myself.

"Damn straight. You walking me out?"

"Don't I always? I can't necessarily do that in your shirt and with you shirtless," I toss over my shoulder as I exit the bathroom. Fletcher grumbles something, except it's muttered under his breath in a way I can't hear the entire statement, only that he's going to spank me. He should know by now that I'm more than okay with his hand landing anywhere on my body, and it's not a punishment either.

Chapter 17
Delilah

"This is a pleasant surprise," Dad greets me when I walk through his door without knocking. I figured since it was open, it means he's not too busy. After I saw Fletch off to work this morning, I went back inside for a few minutes. There were a few things I needed to pick up as well as make sure the toaster was unplugged. Then I was grabbing my purse and heading to the garage to go back to my place. The quick showers I've been having with Fletch meant that the minute I stepped through my door at home, all I had to do was change into my work clothes and get to work.

Today was an easy one. I only had two accounts to work on. So, once those were settled, I made a phone call to my mom asking what was on Dad's agenda. She let me know he was at the station today. We chit-chatted for a few minutes, with her asking me about work and me asking her about what she's been up to, and then we made plans to grab lunch this weekend and go to Peach Springs annual garage sale. I'm still looking for that elusive office chair. I doubt I'll find one this weekend, but it would be a good time to find a few other things for my place, too. After our call, I changed again back into a bra and panties while second-guessing the outing. The fact of the matter is, I really hate undergarments, yet I'd never not wear them around my dad. Plus, Fletcher would lose his mind if he found out, especially if he wasn't with me while doing so. An idea comes to fruition. Once we're out in the open but there's no more keeping our relationship a secret, and none of this the-Chief's-daughter-is-off-limits business, I can make it happen. Fletcher would absolutely love me for it, but that's the best part. I'll make sure to wear one of my dresses he loves so much, leave the bra and panties at home for the night. Once we're sitting down for dinner, I'll take his hand in mine and place it on my thigh. Fletcher would do the rest, slowly slide the tips of his fingers up my skin, I'd open my legs for him, and he'd feel exactly how bare and wet I am for him. I could also give him a little peep show, but that would require being very strategic, and I'm not sure I could pull it off without flashing someone or falling over.

"I was in the area and figured I'd stop in and say hello." I move closer inside. I've got Dad's beloved fountain drink in my hand, buttering him up, so to speak.

"Well, I'm glad you did. Is that for me?" He points at the Styrofoam cup in my hand. I had to get gas, and I've already met my quota of caffeine for the day, but Dad lives off it, and I knew he'd be all too happy to indulge in more.

"It is, extra ice, too." I stir it around. "Door open or closed?" I ask before walking further into his office.

"Closed. Those knuckleheads out there are liable to barge in here and interrupt," Dad states. The last time I was here, it was him doing the charging to introduce me to the guys who didn't work here before I left for college. When I came home, there wasn't a lot of time. I'd visit with my parents and extended family when they were near. Dad would try to be home more, which meant the station stops were few and far between. Obviously, that led to kissing Fletch the first time as well.

"We all know you love them, you big ole' softy." I hand him his beloved soda, Mountain Dew, and he has no problem acting like the big goofball he is.

"Shh, don't tell any of them that." He takes a healthy swig of his drink, acting like he hasn't had a fountain drink in forever.

"Did I bring you a drink Mom and your doctor told you to stay away from?" I side-eye him, my arms folded over my chest, ready to snatch it out of his hands if that's the case.

"Sit down and take a load off. And for your information, Nosy Rosy, the doctor said to cut back, not cut out. I'm down to one or two of these a week." He's proud of himself, which can only mean one thing. There's a health-related reason.

"Dad, you want to tell me the reason why you're cutting back?" His office vibe is dark and moody. Dark brown wood paneling, wood bookcases, and wood desk add to the vibe. There's a television mounted to the wall on one side of his desk, and the other is stacked with books and files. Behind his desk Dad has awards, a framed insignia of Peach Springs Police Department, and a few pictures. One with him and the mayor, another with Mom at a fancy dinner, and then me in my cap and gown graduating from college.

"The doctor says my A1C is high." Great, I'm the culprit in helping his sugar soar.

"High or borderline?" I question. He doesn't take his health seriously enough.

"Not borderline, but enough to where he's having me prick my finger before every meal and document each time. Depending on what he sees and my next lab appointment, we'll go from there. So no, you don't need to call your mother. I've been cutting back." I'll still call her. I get that the two of them have one another, but I'd have liked to have a little insight, too.

"Fine, but I'm not bringing you another soda, and I'm damn sure not bringing you anything from the bakery." I slide my hands down the back of my dress before taking a seat. Dad's office may be man cave-ish, but at least his chairs are comfortable, plush, and deep, wrapping around your body like a hug. My eyes land on a piece of paper with Fletcher's name on it, and my Spidey senses instantly go on alert.

"Not even once in a blue moon?" he asks, seeing where my eyes are locked on the sheet of paper.

"No way. I want you around for a good long while." I sit down finally. "What's that?" There are a few other names following Fletch's.

"Annual reports, promoting, demoting, and giving the boot. Thankfully, no one is getting the latter. Wild is being promoted from sergeant to lieutenant. About damn time, too. The man is better than Wyatt and George put together. Obviously, this doesn't leave this room." Now I'm going to have to explain to Fletch that we need to keep this between the two of us a bit longer without letting on what I know. And doesn't that just suck for me. No way am I going to put a promotion in jeopardy when he's this close to a life-altering career move.

"I won't say a word, but it's going to cost you." I place my hand out, palm out. Some would think I'm asking for money. Dad knows I'm not, and this is also a test to see just how much he's cutting back. How I'm managing not to show the card I've been dealt is beyond me. All I know is I'm sucking it up and making the best of it.

"Damn it, Delilah. You run a hard bargain." Dad opens his desk drawer, where for as long as I can remember he kept a stash of *Lifesavers*.

"Does Mom know you have these still with all of this *I'm cutting back* non-sense?" I air quote him, and I'd like to say I'm surprised when there isn't a hint of remorse in his disposition. It seems he's going to be his own worst enemy if he doesn't start to take his health seriously.

"Yeah, yeah. I hear the same thing from your mother. I'll try to do better." He slaps a full pack of the hard candy in my hand.

"Thank you. I'd appreciate you staying alive for as long as possible. Now, I'm off to run a couple of errands. Love you, Daddy." I stand up and walk around his desk to give him a quick hug and a kiss on the cheek.

"Love you, too, Delilah. Thank you for stopping by. Try to come around more often when you aren't working, alright?" He gives me a tight squeeze.

"How about you do the same? I'm pretty sure I get my workaholic ways from you." I wink.

"I suppose you do." He lets out a soft chuckle.

"There's no supposing. Ask Momma." We finish saying our goodbyes, and then I'm out the office door, closing it behind me. While I'm here, I may as well stop and say hello to my favorite sergeant.

Chapter 18
Fletch

"Were you looking for me?" I come up behind Delilah, whispering in her ear. She might not have seen me when she walked into the station, but I sure as fuck saw her. I was coming out of the breakroom. Wyatt was in there, and I wanted to ask him a question about the case he was working on. After talking to Chief Taylor and doing a standard search on the homeowner's house, he noticed Wyatt had a similar last name on a file for a warrant being served today, a search for drugs with the intent to sell. Since this is a small town, Taylor suggested we cross-reference the welfare check case I've been working. Well, let's just say it seems the apple didn't fall far from the tree. Wyatt's file showed the same first and last name on his report as mine, Marshall Kennedy. I did some quick thinking, pulled up the property appraisers' website, and it seems he owns both properties. Chief Taylor asked the judge to include the other property as well on a hunch since we're not sure which house is his permanent address. Even if the house for the case I'm working is only a rental property like the neighbors suggested, it doesn't mean he's not using one for a stash house. Which means we've got to act fast, and after a taste of Delilah, I'll be heading out with Wyatt to both properties along with a few other officers, including Chief Taylor.

"I'm not sure. It depends on who's asking?" After our talk in the breakroom formulating a plan with Wyatt, I veered toward the locker room to change. My everyday uniform of jeans and a uniform shirt weren't going to cut it for searching a house. I switched into my tactical pants, boots, a black shirt with Peach Springs Police Department on the back and a sheriff's star on the front left pocket. The next step was my duty belt, a spare pair of handcuffs, and my bulletproof vest.

"Woman." I'm damning myself for putting on my vest now. The only way I'm able to feel even a hint of her is because she's pressing her ass into my cock.

"Hmm." She's already lost in the way my hand is dragging up the hem of her dress, the tips of my fingers grazing her upper thighs. I do a quick check, making sure no one is around. I'll be damned if someone else besides me sees my woman. How hot she looks when my fingers are inside her pussy. How wet she gets with each sweep of my thumb along her clit, knowing she likes when I pinch it when we have more time to play. And I'll be damned if someone captures a damn moment of my time when she's giving herself to me completely.

"Walk, Delilah, gotta get us out of the open," I coax her, cradling her thighs with mine as I maneuver us out of the hallway into a room no one uses during the day. The cleaning closet. It's a few feet in front of us, and I've been inside a handful of times to know it'll work in a quick pinch.

"Fletcher." My thumb slides along the apex of her thigh, where I'm sure another pair of lacey confections are covering her wet cunt.

"Almost there. One foot in front of the other." With my hands all over her body, she's going to need to open the door, and I can already tell that's going to be a hard task for her. She's got her head tipped back on my chest, eyes closed, and the only thing she's capable of thinking about is my fingers working her cunt.

"Hmmm." Another prolonged and low uttered sound leaves her throat right as we make it to the closet.

"Door, Delilah." I've got my hands full. My hand on her waist moves upward to cup her tit as my other fingers slide beneath her panties, wetness coating them, and I'm having a hard time refraining from sliding two fingers inside her wet heat.

"Can't," she replies, her hands digging into the outsides of my thighs.

"You either open that door, or you lose me." Neither one of us are ready to let go, but if we don't get inside the closet soon, I'll be getting her off where we could get caught.

"Fletch." I watch as she attempts to grasp the handle. Her body is boneless against mine, and she's having a hard time. And doesn't that just piss me the fuck off.

"Goddamn, all this sweetness just for me." I'm tempted to take my hands off her to help guide us through the door. Except that would require me losing her body, and there's no damn way I'm allowing that.

"More, please."

"Door, Delilah. Now." She finally takes ahold of the knob, twists it, and it opens without so much as making a noise. I do one last glance around us, my left, my right, and even behind me. My head is usually on a swivel, always on alert when I need to be, but when Delilah is like this, it's damn hard.

"Now, please stop teasing me." I slip one finger inside her tightness as we make it inside. Sadly, I have to take my hand off her tit in order to shut and lock the door without it slamming.

"Quiet, baby," I tell her, using the palm of my hand on the door to close it, sliding down the length of it while taking her mouth with mine. I don't stop until I feel the latch on the handle, flicking it in the upwards position to lock, and then we're locked inside the dark room.

"I'm not sure I can," she says, pulling away from my lips, going to my throat, nipping at the skin with her teeth.

"Fuck, I want to watch as you fall apart on my fingers," I groan, adding another digit inside her cunt. I flip the switch next to her head, and the bright fluorescent light shows me every delicate feature of the woman I love.

"Yes, Fletch, more." I lift her thigh over my own, spreading her open.

"You're going to come, hard and fast. Lift your dress, let me watch as I finger-fuck your pussy." After a brief moment of me no longer sliding in and out of her heat but instead holding steady, she does as I want. "You're beautiful, Delilah, and you're all mine." I pick up my pace, pulling out before pushing back in, my thumb pressing on her clit as the tips of my fingers move back and forth, and it's everything Delilah needs and more.

"Fletch." I do the only thing possible to keep others from hearing her come apart for me. I kiss her like my life depends on it, like she's my air to breathe and the blood running through my veins.

"Anyone seen Fletch? We gotta rock and roll, buttholes," Wyatt says outside, and with how close his voice is carrying, I'd bet my damn paycheck he's standing right outside the door. I swear to Christ if this motherfucker so much as jingles the handle, I'm going to come unglued.

Delilah's half-shuttered eyes peel open, the orgasm she's coming down from is gone, and in its place is worry. I shake my head, telling her in not so many ways to keep quiet. My ears stay peeled for his receding footsteps. Once I know the coast is clear, I'll make sure no one will notice my woman leaving the closet looking like she's sexed up. I slowly pull my fingers out of her pussy, feeling the fluttering of her orgasm that still lingers, and I'm not wasting time or the remnants of her coming for me. I bring my fingers to my mouth and let her watch as I lick them clean.

I lose my concentration when she cups my cock in her hand. As much as I hate to stop her, we have to get going. If I'm gone for too much longer, they'll send out a search party, or worse, leave without me. Shit would hit the motherfucking fan. I'd get my ass handed to me, chewed up and down, and everywhere in between, get written up, the whole nine yards.

"Later, sweetheart, promise," I whisper into her ear, stepping closer and placing a kiss on the column of her throat. Plus, everyone knows the adrenaline rush from coming off a kickass day makes sex ten times hotter.

"You're sure?" she replies. Delilah is all about

giving what she gets. Love that about my woman, but right now, the last thing I need is to have her mouth wrapped around my cock when I need to be mission focused.

"Positive. Tonight, when I get home, I want you naked and cuffed in my bed. I'll fuck your tits, then I'll fuck your mouth." I pull back wanting to see if she's up for another round in handcuffs. Sure enough, she's more than ready. Match fucking made.

"Text me when you're on your way. I'll be ready and waiting." Son of a bitch, there's no way I'm leaving her without another taste of her lips.

"Fuck, yeah," I murmur before my mouth is on hers. Delilah opens with one sweep of my tongue along the seam of her lips. I swallow down the soft little purr she gives me each and every time we have a moment like this. My hand clenches around her neck, holding her exactly where I want her as I take from her. This kiss is going to have to hold me over. These things take hours, which means getting home at my usual time is out the window. I'll be lucky to get off by early nightfall.

"I love you, Fletcher Wild. Come home to me." Delilah Taylor has been around the block a few times with her father being a police chief. I imagine she's seen him dressed down and dressed in gear.

"Love you, Delilah. No one can keep me away from coming back to you." It's a promise I'm making here and now. The other questions that are lingering in the air can wait until later. "Come on, let's get you out of here." She nods but remains quiet. Yeah, we're going to be coming back to a much-needed discussion, and very fucking soon.

Chapter 19
Fletch

"**E**veryone have their comms in?" I ask over the channel. We're at the second house. The whole team came together for today's festivities. The last house was a clean sweep. No one was there except for a shit ton of drugs, paraphernalia, and enough illegal guns to supply a cartel. We called in the drug enforcement agency to help process everything and to move this along in order for us to get to the second search warrant.

"Go for Joyfield," Wyatt says.

"Good for Matthers," George responds.

"Landry here," another officer from night shift says into his communication device. We finish going down the line with the rest of the officers we have on the house. DEA decided to wrangle up a few of their officers to make it a mutual effort since the amount we found at the last house was as big as it was. Still, I'm taking lead, and it's up to me when we barge through the front door.

"Warwick is a go," Chet checks in.

It's go-time. "Peach Springs PD, open up!" I bang on the door. "Search warrant!" I finish off, letting them know who's at the door. I'd rather not break the door down, and sometimes it comes down to it. Everyone is aware of the report I wrote up indicating a child and likely her mother have been seen here.

I repeat the process one more time, waiting for a response, and when none is received, and we're about to use the battering ram, I yell out, "Stop!" The door slowly creeps open. It only opens an inch, and where I should be met eye to eye, I have to lower my gaze, slow and steady like. There are still too many unknown variables I can't control. Being lead on this doesn't help the knots of worry in my gut when I'm confronted with a pair of big blue eyes and a wobbly bottom lip. Fuck me running, this day has gone from good to bad in a blink of any eye.

"Is your momma here?" I bend down, going against every protocol we've ever been taught. There's no way I'm aiming my fist, a gun, or a battering ram in her face. It's clear as day she's been crying.

"Momma?" The little girl opens the door another inch.

"Wyatt, cover me," I toss over my shoulder, squatting down until I'm on my haunches, hoping being on eye level will make the little girl trust me.

"Do you know where she is?" Her head shakes back and forth, and tears start to stream down her cheeks. "That's okay. You want to come out here? We'll help you find her." As much as I'd love to open the door and pick her up swiftly, there are too many variables. I'd like to say no one would leave what I'm assuming is a toddler home alone, but you never know. What I'm more worried about is someone coaxing her to open the door and setting a trap. I watch as she plops her thumb in her mouth, nods, and she takes a step closer to me.

"Wild." Warwick has a warning tone in his voice over the comm, and I know I've got seconds to spare before shit goes further south than it already has. I hear it before I see it. I make a split decision hoping I'm not injuring the officer but knowing there's no way I won't protect this little girl.

"I hear it. Come on, sweetheart, we'll find your momma." I push the door open a few extra inches until my hands wrap around her tiny body, pulling her into my chest, and barely clear out before the sound of guns cocking overwhelm the need to get the fuck out of the way. The little girl lets out a loud scream. My hand cups the back of her head, pulling her into my chest wishing like hell there were more protection surrounding us.

"Go, go, go!" Landry bellows through the comm. The second my back is turned to the door, I double-time my pace, running while having a gun strapped to my shoulder and a kid in my arms. The only hope we have is the shields the rest of the team has surrounding the house. I'm nearing where we've got our vehicles parked when a bullet whirs past me. I zig then zag in my pursuit to get us out of the fucking line of fire. The next gunshot, I'm not so lucky. I feel the burn, heat, and pain. Through it all, I don't stutter in my steps. I push on.

"It's okay. You're okay." I keep my voice as calm as possible. Her screams can be heard over the fight going on behind us. My feet eat up the pavement, trying to move in different ways to avoid another hit.

"Get down!" Taylor screams in my ear. I don't know if he's talking to the rest of the crew or me. It doesn't matter. I duck, dipping and weaving like a bobber in the water when a fish is caught on your hook. The vehicle is in reach. I turn the corner, and that's when I'm hit again. This time, my knees buckle from the impact of being shot.

"Motherfucker," I mutter, somehow managing to drop, tuck, and roll in order to take the brunt of the fall while keeping the little girl secured in my arms. Taylor or one of the other agents grabs me by my arms, pulling me along the concrete. Unfortunately, it's the same damn area where I got shot. There's no amount of breathing through the pain. The adrenaline from the day decides to drain from me, because the last thing I remember is feeling someone taking the toddler out of my arms and me holding the fuck on.

Chapter 20
Delilah

"Where is he?" I come flying through the automatic doors of the emergency room, running right toward Asher to ask my question. I received a call less than ten minutes ago from Fletch's older brother, telling me to get to the hospital. An ambulance was enroute with the man I love. I didn't bother changing, still in my work clothes, forgoing putting on a bra, and instead grabbing my zip-up hoodie, sliding my feet in a pair of leather clog shoes before running out the door. Literally. I'm not even sure how I drove, if I obeyed the speed limit signs or if my car is parked straight. All I cared about was getting to Fletch.

"In an emergency room being worked on. We don't know much. Waiting for your dad to come back and give us an update," Beau says. Madelyn moves closer to Asher, comforting him. God, what I wouldn't give to have another moment with Fletch before we parted ways hours upon hours ago. I should have known today would be dangerous. I'd never stand in his way from doing a job he loves. What I would have done is kiss him one more time, hug him one more time, and tell him I love him one more time.

"My dad?" I close my eyes, stopping in my tracks of running to the reception area. Of course, Dad was with his men. He'd never sit back and let the younger guys do this on their own.

"He's okay. Everyone else is, too. Fletch was the only officer down. Not sure on what all is involved. We were told to wait here," Asher states. I can see the toll it's taking on him and Beau to hold back and not bang down doors. The similar can be said for myself, except there's something I can do about it.

"I'm calling my dad. This is bullshit." I whip my phone out of my jacket pocket, unlock the device, and go through my recent calls until I land on *Dad*. I press his name and bring the phone to my ear.

"Kind of busy right now, Delilah," Dad answers after the first ring.

"Well, get un busy and come update Fletcher's family and bring me to the man I love," I blurt out. The whole emergency room is listening in, I'm sure. Who fucking cares? My only concern is lying in a hospital bed right now, and I have no idea if he's dying or not.

"Son of a—" Dad says. "Fletch, you good with Delilah coming back here?" I hear him ask. He doesn't sound surprised or upset in the least.

"Give me the phone," Fletch says with a groan. I can hear the rustle of paper beneath him. I cock my hip out, tapping my foot on the linoleum floor, and slowly lose my patience. The need to scream is hitting me hard right now. Maybe I should hit my phone on something hard until I get answers as well.

"Fletcher, please tell me you're okay, or I'm going to jump over the receptionist desk, hit the button, and come back there to find you myself." I'm being a bit extra, but I couldn't give two fucks.

"Delilah, I'm okay. Hell of a way to spill the beans to your dad, sweetheart." His voice deep and raspy. God, the way I love to hear him talk.

"Oops," I reply.

"Walk to the receptionist, and grab the family, too. I'd rather talk about this in one fell swoop, then he can tell the masses. I'll call my bud up in Wyoming, and maybe you can break me out of this place sooner rather than later." His voice is strong and steady, calming the nerves swirling throughout my nervous system.

"Alright, hold, please." I move my phone away from my cheek. "Asher, Mads, Beau we're being summoned. The good news is he's talking without exertion. The bad news is he's making us wait until we're all back there to tell us everything." They walk with me toward the reception desk, where I'm sure we'll have to hand over identification, which I'm lacking. Apparently, when I rolled in on two wheels, the only thing I grabbed were my keys and phone. I don't even know if my purse is in my car or still on the couch in the living room.

"Take your time, sweetheart. I'm not going anywhere." His voice helps calm my nerves while I overanalyze everything and anything. Like how I'm usually Delilah or woman. Twice now he's used the sentiment *sweetheart*, and twice it's given me a sense of security.

"We're here," I tell him once all three of us are where he told us to go.

"Hand the phone to Claire. I'll do the rest." Fletch is always in control even from a hospital bed.

"Hi, Claire, Fletcher Wild would like to talk to you." I hold the phone out to her. My father probably could have been out here in the same amount of time. That's not how Fletch works. Everyone knows he's a man who takes care of business in every way possible. I watch and listen to the one-sided conversation. She's multi-tasking while saying yes, clicking on a few things with her mouse while glancing from me to her computer.

"Yes, sir, I'll walk them back now. Badges are already printed. You're welcome." Claire hands me my phone back. Seeing the screen is void of the call, I take it from her and pocket it in my jacket. "Here you go. These are your temporary badges for you to go back and see him. We're only supposed to let in two at a time, but we're bending the rules for one of our own." She has four badges, one on each finger, for us to place on our clothes.

"Thank you. I appreciate everything you've done for Fletch and us," I tell her as I clip the badge on my jacket.

"You're welcome. I'll buzz you through. Chief Taylor will be waiting for you on the other side." At least Dad isn't injured, too. I'm not sure how I'd be able to handle two of the men who mean the most to me being hurt. The four of us walk together again. I'm trying to keep my pace slow and steady when what I'd really like to do is run. I've never been in this situation before. Dad, for the most part, never had an incident like this, at least none that I was aware of. Sure, he'd been shot at, but his bulletproof vest protected him. He'd come home after a medic would look over him, take a couple of days off, show off the bruise, and pretend like everything was okay.

The moment the doors open, Dad is standing off to the side. He must know what I need. His arms wrap around me, my head hits his chest, and I'm letting out silent tears while he holds me. "Oh, Delilah, he's okay, you're okay. Though, I've got some questions."

"I'm sure you do," I joke. It's time to pull myself

together. There isn't time for tears or fears. Fletch will be okay, he has to be okay, and no matter what happens, I'm going to be with him, forever.

"Come on, let's get you all back to Fletcher. He's crawling out of his skin as it is." Dad guides me until his arm is wrapped around my shoulder. I remain quiet while he says hello to Beau, Asher, and Madelyn. Thankfully, he's doing all of this while walking down the long corridor, the noise of machines, the chatter coming from each room, the bustling of nurses and doctors. My eyes swing from left to right, looking for Fletch, when we stop outside a door. There he is, on the bed, shirt off, a bandage on his neck and on his arm, blood saturating one. I'm standing stone-cold still. I'm about to crumble. He could be in so much worse shape. Mentally, I know this, but tell that to my damn heart.

"Woman." One word. Fletch says one word, and it means more than I'd have ever imagined.

Chapter 21
Fletch

"I don't know where to touch you." Delilah comes to an abrupt halt after finally moving her ass into the room. Really, this is overkill, but it's also how things work in an emergency department with a shit ton of reports that need to be written. Luckily, the little girl is okay. She's back in her mom's possession. The damn report is going to be eight inches thick by the time everything is said and done. A welfare check turned into a drug distributor case. Marshall Kennedy Senior and Junior are now behind bars. The little girl, whose name is Emory, and her mom, Cassidy, are together. Marshall, the older of the duo, was holding Emory over Cassidy's head, holding her hostage until she did the drop he demanded. Emory's dad, the younger of the two Marshalls, wasn't much better. Strung out on his own product, he did and went along with everything his father wanted. It was a shit situation that only turned shittier. The last I heard, Cassidy's mom, Jackie, is on her way to Peach Springs, and hopefully, she takes her daughter and granddaughter back home with her. They both deserve a clean break and to find some good after the hell they've been through.

"Come here, Delilah. You won't hurt me." I lift up my good arm, ready to have her next to me. She needs it, and fuck if I don't need it. The last thought I had before I passed out was not making good on my promise to come home to her. I can't say I'm too happy about falling to my damn knees with a baby in my arms, but I guess it happens with how much blood I had lost from the shot to my arm.

"I'm not getting in bed with you, Fletcher Wild. Your family is here, and so is my dad," she whisper-hisses. Beau lets out a chuckle, letting on that he heard her. I narrow my eyes, and he raises his hands in defeat. That's right, fucker. I love my brothers, love all of them, but I'll beat their asses if they so much as hurt Delilah from laughing at her antics.

"Woman, sit your ass down and give me your eyes." I'd be on my way home already if it weren't for my arm, a through and through by a high caliber rifle. Fucking bullets from an AR-15. I'm lucky the bullet didn't stay lodged inside my arm.

"Fine." My hand reaches for hers the second her

ass meets the bed, and she's sitting near my hip. So close I can smell her, yet I want her closer. Always do and always will.

"Closer." She leans down. I lick my lips, and her eyes darken with need. "I'm okay. Once they do an X-ray, the doctor will stitch me up, and then we can go home, alright?"

"Home," she repeats.

"Yeah." I lift up, pressing my lips to hers in a quick kiss, too fucking quick, but like she's said, we've got an audience, and I'm not about to embarrass her.

"Alright, you two lovebirds. The nurse is about to take you to X-ray. We'll wait in here for you." Chief Taylor doesn't say a word about Delilah and me. Probably because I gave him a quick rundown before he went to meet everyone. I laid it out, told him I loved her, and it was the real deal, marriage and kids. Taylor pretty much said we'd talk later and to worry about getting better first. I'm not too worried about how the conversation will go. He had his chance to make my injury worse, and he didn't take it. Therefore, I'm thinking he's on board with me dating his daughter.

"I'm going with him," Delilah states. I don't have the heart to tell her any differently.

"She's good," I tell Taylor over her shoulder.

"Alright, well, now that we've had our eyes on you, we're going to head home. Answer your phone. Colton sent a text, and Owen said he'll call you once you're home and settled," Asher states.

"Delilah, we'll go to Fletch's and change the sheets and stock the fridge, if that's okay with you?" Madelyn asks her best friend instead of me. I'm more than okay with that, going as far to hold back my smirk. I'm not an asshole to my brother's woman, but I also understand the reason she's asking Delilah. She's making sure she won't walk in on anything we don't want her to see.

"I'd appreciate that so much, thank you," Delilah responds.

"Will you hand me my phone? I'm pretty sure after they manipulate my arm, stitch me up, and do whatever else they want, I'm gonna be wiped," I ask Beau.

"Not a bad idea. You good?" Beau has been in the family house the longest, didn't seem set on anything in particular so far, and that's okay. No one said he needed to settle down as young as our parents did.

"I'm good. Appreciate you coming out." I wrap my palm around my phone.

"Not a problem. Holler if you need anything." We nod at one another, then he backs away and heads for the door.

I glance down at my phone and see Colt's message.

> Colt: You good?

> Me: I am. Got Delilah here with me, and I know she'll be taking care of me.

> Colt: Don't know how you do it. Variety is the spice of life.

> Me: You think that until you find a good one. Thanks for checking in. See you soon?

> Colt: I'll be over tomorrow, let the masses come over first, then I'll stop by.

> Me: Sounds good.

"Mr. Fletcher, are you ready?" The nurse walks in with a damn wheelchair.

"Yep. Is that necessary? I can walk." It's not like they took me out by my legs.

"Afraid so. It's hospital policy," she replies.

"Fine." Delilah stands up first, moving out of the way but never out of reach. I get it. If roles were reversed and she were shot, you couldn't pry me away from her. Fuck, I don't want to now as it is. I sit my ass in the wheelchair, annoyed at the circumstance of being wheeled around on display. This shit can't be done soon enough. I'm ready to go home, lay my ass down, and hold my woman. Delilah must sense my thoughts, she keeps her hand in mine as she walks beside me, and holds my hand. Now I'm going to have to convince her come tomorrow that I'll be completely back to normal even if I'm off work while they wrap up the investigation. I know exactly how to kill time while I'm off for the time being, and it's going to be with my woman handcuffed to the bed.

Chapter 22
Fletch

"On the bed, flat on your back, hands above your head, feet planted on the mattress, and spread your legs." We just got out of the shower, both of us naked, and I'm tired of waiting to have Delilah like this. She's been denying me every chance she gets, thinking I'll pull a stitch in my arm, or my neck will start bleeding. Neither of which will happen. They're healing, and I've only got a few days left of my week off.

"Fletcher." My name tumbles off her lips. Just when I think she'll try to stop this from happening, she turns her back toward me and crawls up the bed.

"Fuck, yeah." I keep my eyes on her heart-shaped ass, seeing a peek of her glistening pussy with each move she makes. I'm biding my time until she's in position before I move to grab my cuffs, making good on my promise.

"If you hurt yourself, I'm going to be so pissed off at you, Fletcher Wild," she says as she rolls onto her back, lifts her arms up, and spreads her legs. I move away from the bed for a minute, going to the dresser and grabbing the cuffs.

"I'm not gonna re-injure myself. Three more days until the stitches will be out, and all of this will be behind us." I've seen the worry she carries on her shoulders, trying to hide it when I'm not looking. Delilah Taylor is strong, sometimes too strong. She's got a damn hard time asking for help, and I'm hoping after today, she'll see we've fucking got this.

"Alright." She takes a steadying breath. The clinking of the metal is the only noise in the room. It doesn't take too much to wrap them around her pretty wrists, and of course, when I climb on the bed to lock her in place, my woman takes advantage.

"Christ, wrap your lips around my cock, woman." I tell her what I want. Since she's dying for a taste of my dick, who am I to deny either one of us? The minute she's locked how I want her. I could pull my cock out of her mouth and fuck her how I want. The only problem with that is I'd be doing a disservice to myself.

"Hmm," she murmurs, hollowing her cheeks, the flat of tongue hitting the underside of my shaft, and I watch as she takes a deep breath before taking me all the way to the back of her throat. My hand cups the back of her head, holding her hair and keeping her steady, trying my hardest not to push her any further than she's able to handle.

"Not gonna last." It's a damn shame to take away this feeling. But since she was adamant that no sex was happening until I was completely recovered, that means I'm fucking ready to go.

"I don't care either way." She pulls off for a moment. Her saliva leaves a trail from her sucking my cock.

"Want your pussy this time. Next time, you can finish me off by swallowing." She never got on birth control, and I'm not complaining one bit. Delilah hasn't had time. I haven't brought it up, and she hasn't either. Whatever happens, happens. I only know I'm not ever wearing a condom with her ever again.

"Fine, if you insist." She swipes at the drop of precum on the tip of my dick.

"Goddamn, I love your mouth." I get off the mattress for a moment. "Your shoulders alright?"

"Yes, I'd be better if you we're closer." She spreads her legs wider, a task I thought was impossible, yet here she goes, surprising me further.

"Working on it, woman." I wedge myself between her spread thighs, my cock lying heavy along her wet slit.

"Not fast enough." She gets sassy in certain areas

of our life. In bed is one of them. It's a fire I'll never put out. Fuck, I'll kindle the damn thing if it starts to fizzle out.

"I hear you, Delilah. Keep your eyes on me." The minute her light blue eyes land on mine, I pull my hips back and drag the underside of my cock along her clit. My hands grip the backs of her legs, lifting them up while moving closer until the tops of my thighs are helping me hold her open.

"Fletch, please." She is fucking perfection. Her long loose hair is a tangled mess, lips plush and full after she's been biting on her bottom lip. Delilah's chest is heaving, hard-as-fuck nipples, and her blush is blossoming on every inch of her naked body.

"You asked for it." I push inside her tight wet heat with one thrust, holding myself still while we both take a moment to breathe. "Good?" I check on her again.

"So good." That's all she has to say. I move, backwards and forwards, rolling my hips, and this may be faster than I'd like it to be, but with the velvet clutch of her cunt, there's not much I can do but fuck her through both of our orgasms. And that's exactly what I'm going to do, each and every time I have her in my arms, forever.

Epilogue
Delilah

One Month Later

"Fletcher," I groan his name. We're at the range. It's been his mission to watch me practice shoot my gun. He's been back at work for three weeks now, and my worry has not ebbed whatsoever. My phone stays next to me the entire day, the ringer on, always, and I'm still having a hard time not jumping when an alert comes through. Fletch wasn't majorly hurt. I know this. I tell myself this daily. I've talked to him, my mom, and my dad. Yet I still worry, and I'm pretty sure it's going to take time to calm my ever-present nerves. Dad even sat down with me after we got the stern talking to of *'You don't have to hide your relationship behind my back. If I could have picked a man for you, it would have been Fletcher Wild.'* Anyways, Dad came over last week, told me to finish up my work, and we were going for coffee and a stroll downtown. We talked. I told him my fears, and he told me Mom had similar fears. Dad explained the only person who could overcome the thoughts plaguing me was myself. He suggested instead of going right to work when Fletch does, to go for a walk, have coffee with Madelyn or Mom, hit up a store, or finally take out the puzzle I hadn't gotten to. Basically, he told me to keep my mind occupied besides work, and so far, it's helped.

"Woman, take your shot," Fletch croons in my ear. God, his voice. It reminds me of how he woke me up this morning, his head buried between my thighs, fingers sliding in and out of my wet center while his mouth was wrapped around my clit. My hands went to the back of his head, holding him to my pussy as I rode out my orgasm. Once I came down from getting my own, I tried to reciprocate, but Fletch wasn't having it. He crawled out of bed, naked as the day he was born, walked into the shower, and told me to get ready for a day out.

"You act like it's easy when your body is this close." When he said to get ready, he left out the important part about where we were going. I opted for another one of my sundresses and left my panties and bra at home. Usually, I'd at least wear a pair of panties, but since Fletcher would be with me all day, I knew it wouldn't be a bad idea.

"You can do it." His hands glide up the inside of my legs. How he managed to secure the outdoor facility without others, I'm not sure. "Show me what you got, Delilah, then I'll bend you over and fuck you like I wanted to this morning." I spread my legs wider, giving him more room, and when he feels my wet pussy, he keeps up talking, making it that much harder to concentrate. "No fucking panties. I should have known. You want my fingers or my cock?" I'm not sure if he actually wants an answer. The hiss of a zipper tells me I'm probably right as he plunges two fingers inside my pussy. The gun in my hand is locked and loaded, ready for me to fire at the paper target.

"Fletcher, you keep fucking me with your fingers, I'm liable to shoot you instead of the target." My arms are out, gun in my right hand, finger on the barrel until I'm ready to fire, and my left hand is cupping the stock of the gun.

"You're close already. Take a deep breath and shoot, Delilah." The heel of his palm sets my clit on edge along with the pumping of his fingers. My body quivers from the inside out, and there's no way breathing can even be accomplished with all the ministrations he's doing to my body.

"Fine." I pry my eyes open, put my finger on the trigger, and fire the gun. Fletch doesn't let up. He flicks his fingers inside me while pulling in and out, keeping his palm pressed on my clit. I don't quit shooting through it all. Even with sweat trickling down my spine and my eyes threatening to close, I keep going.

"Goddamn, that's sexy as hell," he says. The gun clatters to the table, my hands reach out for leverage, and I roll my hips. "Stop." I was so close, so damn close.

"I'm going to murder you," I groan when he pulls his fingers out of me. Taking my orgasm away is fucking cruel.

"No, you're not." I'd fight with him over that statement, except I feel him pushing up the skirt of my dress. He kicks my feet out wider, and that's when I know I'm about to get more than his fingers. I'm going to get his thick cock, and I hope to God he doesn't go gentle. Not with the mood I'm in. The teasing was too much. Him eating me earlier without being able to return the favor annoyed me even more.

"Fuck me," I demand.

"I am. You're awfully impatient today, Delilah." His hands grip the sides of my hips, his cock is notched at my entrance, and I push back.

"Stop teasing me, Fletcher Wild, or I'll use my own damn fingers." I'm pushing him, which could backfire. He could very well make me wait longer or pull away completely and make me wait until we get back home.

"I'm done teasing you. I'm doing this while I'm

buried inside you, Delilah. I'm not asking; I'm telling. We're getting married. I've got the ring. All you have to do is put my ring on."

"Yes!" He thrusts to the hilt, burying himself completely inside of me. "Yes, I'll marry you." My head drops down, and tears are streaming down my cheeks in happiness, content, and sheer freaking joy. Fletch couldn't have made this day any better if he tried.

"Fuckin love you, love fuckin' you, and gonna love you the rest of our fuckin' lives." He pulls my body up, dips his knees, and keeps moving in and out of my body while bringing us closer together.

"And I love you." It's a statement and a promise all rolled into one. One I'm going to keep forever with Fletcher by my side.

Epilogue
Fletch

Two Months Later

"I'm sorry the test was negative," Delilah says quietly. We're back in Wyoming. She's getting the tattoo she's always wanted but couldn't settle on it until recently. Lawson is in the back room adding on to his sleeve. This time, it's going from his upper arm into his chest. Abe, a cousin to the Johnson Brothers, is the only guy I'd trust with Delilah's ink as well as my own.

"Woman, I'm not with you for your baby making capabilities. Sure, I'd love nothing more than to see you pregnant with our child, and when it happens, it happens." Her shoulders lower from her ears, and she takes a deep breath. I should have fucking seen the signs. This shit has been weighing on her for far too long. Delilah isn't nervous about the tattoo she's getting down the length of her spine. She is worried something is wrong with her when it very well could be a me thing, too. Hell, it could be it's not the right time. We aren't married yet, which I'm changing this fucking weekend. We'll get our tattoos, tell Lawson bye, and head toward a small cabin an hour outside of Arrowleaf, Wyoming. Tomorrow, I'll give her the surprise of a century, one I've been working on with Marigold night and day. My woman is indecisive as fuck—the date, the dress, the venue, the guest list, it's endless. I'm tired of not having Delilah tied to me in a way she'll carry my last name.

"Fletcher." She closes her eyes, slowly taking another breath before showing me her gorgeous baby blues. "Will you make me a deal?"

"Name it."

"We give this a couple of more months, but if it doesn't happen naturally, we go to the doctors and figure things out. I still want children. Adopting wouldn't be outside of my scope. Would it be yours?" It's a heavy subject. I'd have no problem either way, kids or no kids.

"They'd still be our children, so no. I've got no problem with adopting. I'm going to say one thing, and you may not like it, but I'll say it anyways. We'll go with whatever avenue we have to. We won't borrow trouble, and definitely not at the expense of your mental health." She nods in understanding and agreement. The shit I've heard at the station, how marriages go through the wringer, relationships turn to shit, I don't want us to become bitter, or to play the blame game. "Alright?"

"Yes, thank you." My hand cups the back of her neck. I bring our foreheads together, letting her see exactly how I feel about her.

"You don't gotta thank me. Love you, Delilah. I'll do anything for you even if that means protecting you in a way you won't like." She opens her mouth, and I dip my head, mouth dipping to hers. I pull on her bottom lip with my teeth, she softly whimpers, and then I'm taking from her, uncaring we're in public. She needs to know right in this moment she's worth every fucking thing to me. My tongue works its way inside her mouth until hers is chasing mine while my eyes remain locked on hers, watching as her lids shutter closed.

A throat clears, and she pulls back fast. Damn, my woman makes me feel alive. Like we were making out in a car on a deserted highway and got caught by her dad.

"Your turn, bud," Lawson says. He's walking without a shirt on, and I'm about to knock him the fuck out.

"Put a damn shirt on." I stand up, my hand reaching for Delilah's to help her do the same.

"Worried your woman likes what she's seeing?" This cocky motherfucker.

"Knock it the fuck off. The only blood allowed in my shop is from tattooing. You two wanna fight like goddamn idiots, take it out back," Abe interjects.

"Fletch, Lawson, I'd really like to get my tattoo now. I mean, if you all are done with your alpha he-man business, that is." Lawson and I haven't ever fought— we talk shit, giving as good as we get—but there's a first time for everything.

"We're good, darlin'. I'm heading out. I gotta wake up with the damn chickens anyways." Lawson holds his hand out for me to shake. I take it and see the glint in his eyes. Fucker knew exactly what he was doing.

"Abe, you get my email I sent you with the design I have in mind?" I've got another surprise up my sleeve. While I'm waiting on his response, I watch as Lawson puts his shirt on and then gives Delilah a quick kiss on the cheek. Dickhead.

"Yep, it's all drawn out. Let me show Delilah what I came up with." She wants a line of peach blossoms down the length of her spine. It's going to be hot as fuck, especially with my hand wrapped around her hair as I take her from behind.

"What are you getting done?" she asks.

"You'll see." I've got zero tattoos where I want my next one placed. Her name is going to be tattooed over my heart, where it'll be every day of our lives.

"Not fair," she pouts.

"You'll like it when it's done." I wink.

"Fine. Hold my hand?"

"Anytime." My fingers entwine with hers, and we follow Abe back to his workspace.

"Later, Abe," Lawson tosses over his shoulder.

"Later," Abe responds. He's already in the zone. His area is clean from working on Lawson, and he's pulling out the hand drawn tattoo for Delilah to approve.

"Oh, wow, it's gorgeous." My gaze is locked on hers. She's looking at the drawing. There's a reason why I've got no problem taking a trip back here whenever I want new ink. I also like to check in with my family away from family.

"Alright, I'll step out. Shirt and bra off, face down on the table." I look up to the ceiling, waiting until Abe has cleared the room and closed the door.

I hear the whoosh of Delilah's clothes and count to five in my head. *One, two, three, four, five.* The fabric meets my chest as I look down at her. "I'm not sure why you insist on keeping a drawer full of bras when you barely wear them, and just so you know, when we get back to the hotel, I'm going to spank your ass." I cup her breasts, thumbs sliding over her pebbled tips, giving her a tease of what's to come.

"Promise?"

"It's a guaran-fuckin-tee." I pinch both of her

sweet-as-cherry nipples, then give her a quick kiss before dropping my hands. "On the table." She'd drop to her knees and take me in her mouth if I so much as hinted at the idea. Instead, she spins on her heel. My hand meets the underside of her ass, and a loud resounding smack echoes in the small room.

"Fletcher!" she admonishes while climbing onto the table, ass up in the air, and my dick is hard as a fucking rock now.

"Later." She slowly nods then lies down. The sides of her tits are showing, and that won't do. "Lift." I walk toward her, using her shirt she threw at me and tucking it beneath her. Fuck, I should have brought a jacket, then she could wear it backwards. "It's not much, but it'll do. You ready?"

"Yeah." Her hand goes to mine, and I take it while sitting down in front of her.

"Abe!" I call out, ready to get this show on the road. I'm more than ready to see the end result and to show Delilah how permanent she is for me before tomorrow.

"All good?" She nods. "Alright, I'll walk you through what I'm about to do. If you need a break, just let me know. Sound good?" Abe asks.

"Yep." I watch him do his thing while keeping an eye on Delilah, all while thinking about how this time tomorrow, she'll be my wife, have my name, and we'll be on our way to a week-long honeymoon where clothes will be optional. Damn, she'll be sore, and my dick will be raw. It sounds like a great fucking life to me.

PLACEHOLDER

I hope you enjoyed Fletch and Delilah's story and will consider leaving a review. If you'd like a bonus scene of Wild Ride click the link below for more!

Wild Ride Bonus Scene

Want more of the Rowdy Johnson Brothers? You can find Lane and Dean's story below. Coming soon is Lawson and JW's books that are up for pre order!

The Rowdy Johnson Brothers

Coming next is Long & Hard, a step brother romance and will be available April 14th

Amazon

Chapter One

Drena

"Kade," my voice is hesitant and there's a reason for that. Never in my life have I done something so brazen. The loud pipes of a motorcycle could be heard over the tourists chatting and music coming from the bars in the area. Even the waves crashing along the shore were no match for the man on the black and chrome *Harley Davidson*. I stopped, wanting to see the person on what had to be the loudest bike ever in our beach town. On the coast of Florida is a place I never want to leave, New Smyrna Beach. It doesn't matter that we're overrun with tourists most of the time or dating is nearly impossible because the true citizens are retirees. I love this little town, which is probably why when Kade captured my attention when he did.

"You can take it Drena," my back is to the mattress, his mattress. File this away for something I've never done in my twenty-eight years on this planet. Except I watched Kade pull up beside where I was standing, maneuver his bike in a way that you could tell he's done it time and again. I was stunned speechless, no longer was I heading toward the bar to grab a bite to eat along with a margarita. My eyes we're on the man with devilish blue eyes, a tilt of his lips, and a few days growth of a beard and that was only his face. The way Kade's biceps and forearms flexed and pulled on his handlebars, covered in tattoos covering his deep olive skin. Broad shoulders, a stomach that doesn't depict washboard abs but is still thick and ripped with muscle. Solid legs that were incased in jeans, and one tilt of his head had me walking toward him. I didn't even know his name until my ass was planted in the seat behind him. His hand going to my outer thigh, pulling me closer to his body before he announced who he was, and I did the same. After that, he revved his bike, looked over his shoulder, piercing eyes staring into mine for a moment. It felt like he was peering into my soul, seeing ever deep crevice of me, I've kept hidden. Kade pulled out of the parking spot he'd only been in a handful of minutes, and we were heading off.

Now we're at his place and both of us are completely naked. Did I mention I've never done something like this before, I didn't even text my friend, breaking every unspoken girl code or rule known to mankind. Apparently, I'm choosing to live on the wild side tonight.

"Have you seen how big you are?" My legs attempt to close, the palm of Kade's hand holds me steady. His other hand is slowly jacking his cock, up and down with a twist of his wrist. He's long, hard, and pierced. I've had his mouth on mine, him dominating our kiss from the get-go, all I could do was follow his lead. Kade's deft hands on in and my body, thick fingers sliding in and out of my wet center. As for his tongue, well feeling it thrashing my clit is a whole other story. The orgasm he gave me felt like an out of body experience, my thighs were locked on either side of his head, my hands buried in his hair, and I'm pretty sure my scream echoed through Kade's whole house.

"Babe, you can take me," my mouth waters, watching as he works his hand on his cock. I'm beginning to think he kept himself from my viewing pleasure for a reason.

"Are you sure about that, your umm...hardware might prove to be difficult," Kade has a frenum piercing, the thick metal on the underside of his cock is sporting a barbell. Never in my life have I seen one this close up and personal. I'm woman enough to admit I've watched porn and did the research to see what certain piercings were called. Then when I went into the tattoo shop for my appointment only to see exactly where different places on the human body could be pierced. I even thought of getting one of my own except I chickened out and stuck with the cluster of flowers on my lower hip, a discreet enough place my overbearing mother would never see unless I wore a more revealing bathing suit. In which I would never in front of her, no thanks the lecture I'd receive isn't worth it.

"Drena, you haven't known me long enough to trust me but know this. You will soon enough. Trust in this though, I'm not looking to hurt you, wanna fuck your tight cunt and watch as you get off this time," Kade says, the shortened version of my name. One in which isn't used all that much, prim and proper is what I've always been told to strive for. Yet, when Kade says the four letters together, it with a roughness to his tone that has me reaching out for his thighs.

"Okay," his hand comes away from my thigh after a soft squeeze and I watch as he picks the condom up from where he dropped it earlier. Kade rips it open with his teeth, then I'm once again enraptured by the way he slides it down his hard cock, being mindful of his piercing the entire time.

"That's my girl."

"Kade," I wiggle my body down in order to get closer to him, my hands gripping the back of his thighs, tired of waiting, and hoping he's ready to go. Surely, he is, my one orgasm to his none isn't very fair in my mind.

"Fuck, I'm not gonna last long. Next time," Kade promises, the head of his cock is at my entrance, slowly entering me, "Let go, Drena," I'm not sure what he's referring to, my hands on his body or the fact my pussy is currently tightening around him. Almost like I'm afraid to let him in, except I'm not, I'd rather die than lose this feeling, "Hands on your tits, I'll do the rest."

My hands let go of the back of his thighs, slowly I trail the tips of my fingers along the outside of my thighs. His eyes are no longer on mine, they're on what I'm doing to my body, Kade rolls his hips, pressing deeper until he's seated more inside me. He waits, I'm impatient as hell and when he nods at my hands I move faster along the path of my body, cupping the undersides of my breasts.

"Please," I beg, I'm ready to push for more except I'm not sure how that would work with his barbell.

"Waiting on you, Drena, playing with your nipples, imagine it's my hands and my mouth," my thumb and pointer finger wrap around the pebbled tips. It would be so much better if this were Kade's mouth but since I can't have that, I work myself like I would when I'm playing with myself.

"More," Kade must be as antsy as I am. Finally. My eyes were slowly closing when I felt his thumb on my clit, sweeping over it in smooth circles, pressing down and then easing up.

"You're taking me, watch as your cunt takes my dick, Drena," he groans, my gaze goes to where his is locked. I was unprepared for how hot the view would be, the way my pussy is stretching to fit his length, wetness coating me and him. Kade moves his thumb from my clit, going to my tattoo and holding me steady.

"Holy shit," I lift my head up, air depleting my lungs before I take another breath. Kade slides in until I feel his piercing drag along a sensitive part in my body.

"God damn, my girl is tight as fuck," a shiver races up my spine hearing how the possessiveness in his voice, watching Kade's muscles flex and pull. It's hot as hell and my eyes move from where we're connected to his body, committing to memory every single nuance of our time together. He moves, pulling back before sliding back into me, the slight swivel of his hips, the way Kade holds his body still while he does a slow grind. My body is lighting up like a firework that's been set off. I'm a blazing inferno, a moth to the flame and I only want more. I'm completely enraptured with Kade, there's no way staying still while he fucks me is possible. I plant my feet on the mattress, lifting my body up with each thrust he makes.

"Kade," he works faster, our tempo in sync with one another like two dancers in a steady rhythm. Him leading and me following. Jesus, never ever have I felt something this pleasurable, been able to let go as freely, and soar like a bird in the sky. My head falls back to the mattress, hands going to my hair, pulling on it as my orgasm takes over me.

"Take me with you, babe. Fuck my cock with your sweet as hell pussy," his movements, his words, and the way he's looking at me is my undoing. I come apart and through it all Kade doesn't stop. He keeps going, making my orgasm last longer, his piercing only heightening my experience, and god how I'd love to feel it without a condom. On one hard and deep push, he plants himself inside me, Kade's body locks up, allowing me to feel him each spurt of cum he jets inside the rubber he's wearing.

"Hmm," I sigh when he falls to his elbows, bracing himself on either side of my head, a lazy smile tugging at his lips.

"Like that look on my girl, give me a few minutes, we'll have a repeat performance," my legs lift and wrap around his waist, locking around him with my ankles.

"I'm going to need more than a few minutes big guy," his hands go beneath my body, wrapping me up, and my own going to Kade's biceps to hold on.

"Is that right, two orgasms your max?" He asks, dipping his head closer to mine. His question has me pausing, my mind drawing a blank at the last time I've ever gotten off more than once in the past.

"I'm pretty sure with a partner, it'd be once and only once. On my own, two has been my limit," I reply, moving one of my hands off his arms. Just as I'm about to touch the dog tags around his neck his hand captures mine, bringing it to his lips.

"Next round, I want your hands fucking your pussy while your mouth is wrapped around my cock until you orgasm, then I'm going to eat you again, after that you'll get me inside of you to round out your third orgasm." Kade states before lifting off of me, "Gotta take care of the condom. Be right back," his mouth press against mine. Kade's tongue slides along my upper lip, a small gasp infiltrates the quietness in the room and he takes the opportunity to deepen our kiss. What started out as something light, turns hot and heavy. My hands lock in his hair, keeping him close to me, turning this into a full on make out session. He drags his hips lazily in and out of my pussy, spurring me on even further.

"Fuckin' condom. Stay here, just like that, Drena," Kade pulls away, leaving me bare and bereft, somehow managing to do as he asks when all I want to do is run after him. Jesus, I'm hooked and we've only been together once.

Amazon

The Wild Brothers Series

Meet the Wild brothers!
Six of your favorite steamy romance authors are
bringing you a steamy, small town romance each week.
The Wild brothers guarantee a wild time

Wild Temptation by Hope Ford
Wild Ride by Tory Baker
Wild Hopes by Evie Mitchell
On the Wild Side by Megan Wade
Forever Wild by Kara Kendrick
Wild Night by Loni Ree

About the Author

Tory Baker is a mom of two teenagers and a dog mom to one wild and active Weimaraner, Remi. She lives in a small coastal town on the east coast of sunny Florida. Oftentimes you'll find her outside soaking up the rays with at least three drinks surrounding her, a wandering imagination, and a notebook in hand where she's jotting down a plot for her next story. She's a lover of writing happily ever afters with Alpha heroes and sassy heroines.

Sign up to receive her **Newsletter** for all the latest news!

Tory Baker's Bombshells is where you see and hear all of the news first!

Also by Tory Baker

The Rowdy Johnson Brothers

His to Take

His to Please

His to Own

His to Claim

Just A Taste

Long & Hard

Men in Charge

Make Her Mine

Staking His Claim

Secret Obsession

Baring it All

His for the Taking

Needing His Touch

Billionaire Playboys

Playing Dirty

Playing with Fire

Playing With Her

Playing His Games

Playing to Win

Vegas After Dark Series

All Night Long

Late Night Caller

One More Night

About Last Night

One Night Stand

Hart of Stone Family

Tease Me

Hold Me

Kiss Me

Please Me

Touch Me

Feel Me

Diamondback MC Second Gen.

Obsessive

Seductive

Addictive

Protective

Deceptive

Diamondback MC

Dirty

Wild

Bare

Wet

Filthy

Sinful

Wicked

Thick

Bad Boys of Texas

Harder

Bigger

Deeper

Hotter

Faster

Hot Shot Series

Fox

Cruz

Jax

Saint

Getting Dirty Series

Serviced (Book 1)

Primed (Book 2)

Licked (Book 3)

Hammered (Book 4)

Nighthawk Security

Never Letting Go (Easton and Cam's story)

Claiming Her (Book 1)

Craving More (Book 2)

Sticky Situations (Travis and Raelynn's story)

Needing Him (Book 3)

Only His (Book 4)

Carter Brothers Series

Just One Kiss

Just One Touch

Just One Promise

Finding Love Series

A Love Like Ours

A Love To Cherish

A Love That Lasts

Stand Alone Titles

Nailed

Going All In

What He Wants

Accidental Daddy

Love Me Forever

Gettin' Lucky

It's Her Love

Meant To Be

Breaking His Rules

Can't Walk Away

Carried Away

In Love With My Best Friend

Must Be Love

Sweet As Candy

Falling For Her

All Yours

Sweet Nothings Book 3—Tory Baker

Loving The Mountain Man

Crazy For You

Trick— The Kelly Brothers

Friend Zoned

His Snow Angel

223 True Love Ln.

Hard Ride

Slow Grind

1102 Sugar Rd.

The Christmas Virgin

Taking Control

Unwrapping His Present

Tempting the Judge

Naughty Noelle

Acknowledgments

This is about to get very long and very wordy because that's just who I am. I've got so many people to thank and shout out that I hope no one is forgotten. When I set out about change this year, I was all freaking in. I'm extremely fortunate you all are taking this wild ride with me. The depth in these stories it fills my heart up with a joy I lost along the way and my cup couldn't runneth over without your support!

To my kids: A & A without you I'd be a shell of myself. You helped me find myself in a moment of darkness. Thank you for picking up the slack around the house while I was knee deep in this deadline, cooking, cleaning, and taking care of Remi (our big lug of a Weimaraner). I love you to infinity times infinity.

NaShara McClaeb: Ya'll can thank her for that gym scene in Staking His Claim. She still sends me so much inspiration, tells me when my sentences ar run-ons or incomplete. Gives me so much shit about y'all vs ya'll. It's ya'll for this girl by the way. There have been many a conversations we've had about a story. Every time I struggled, she was there to kick my ass into gear. I can't thank you enough! Also, she's my sports partner through and through

Katie Cadwallader (Okay Kyle it's Welter but iykyk): This woman right here is responsible for so freaking much and not just my amazing cover photos. We bounce off each other for ideas, she's the only person I know who is so creative and still have the mindset of a business consultant. Her family has become an extension of mine and I can't wait to see her again!

Mayra: My sprinting partner extraordinaire. Girlfriend, we made it through 2022 ahead of schedule. One day I will fly my butt to California to hug you!

Julia: How do you deal with me and my extra sprinkling of commas? The real MVP, the one who deals with my scatterbrained self, missing deadlines, rescheduling like crazy, and the person I live vicariously through social media.

Amie Vermaas Jones: Thank you for always and I do mean always helping me on my last minute shit. It never fails that I'm sending you an SOS asking for your eyes. Beach days are happening and SOON!

Thank you for being here, reading, not just my books but any Author's stories. We do appreciate you more than you know, the reason why we can live out our dream is for readers, bloggers, bookstagrammers, bookmakers, Authors, and everyone in between.
THANK YOU!

All this to say, I am and will always be forever grateful, love you all!

Printed in Great Britain
by Amazon